STOLEN

TRIBUTE BRIDES OF THE DREXIAN WARRIORS #9

TANA STONE

BROADMOOR BOOKS

ONE

K os rocked back on his heels, dragging a hand through his short brown hair, as he peered out the window of the ship. Slashes of light zoomed by as they cut through the blackness of space, the spaceship flying at warp speed toward their destination.

Even though the computerized beeps and whirring sounds reminded him of the bridge on the space station—casually referred to as the Boat—the Inferno Force ship was worlds away from it. Not that he minded. He found the dimly lit ship with its stripped-down steel interior to be a welcome change from the brightness of the station. This ship was a bit battered, and more than a little bare-bones, but it flew fast and had impressive firepower—both things he was grateful for on the rescue mission.

As a Drexian, he was part of the warrior species known throughout the galaxy as fierce fighters who defended others. Drexians had saved countless worlds from destruction from the violent Kronock. They also defended Earth—unbeknownst to most of the planet's inhabitants—from alien invasion. In return, Earth provided the Drexians, who hadn't produced females in a generation, with brides for their warriors. Tribute brides, they were called. It was one of these Earth brides that Kos was on a mission to rescue. *His* tribute bride.

Not that he'd ever laid eyes on her. He bit his lower lip as he thought about putting off meeting the human when they'd been on the Boat. He'd been an idiot, and now he was paying the price. Of course, he'd never anticipated that she would be kidnapped along with the other new brides or that he would crash land on an alien planet after the station evacuated. Still, he'd wasted his chance and now she was missing. He grunted and slammed a palm against the glass.

One of the Inferno Force warriors spun around and eyed him. "Don't worry. We'll get your tribute back for you."

Kos nodded—remembering that the first officer's name was Kalex—but didn't respond as the soldier with shaggy brown hair and tattoos banding his arms turned back around.

He knew he was lucky to be with the team of Inferno Force warriors sent to locate and rescue the abducted tribute brides and their handlers, but he also knew he didn't belong with the edgy fighters. Where he followed protocol, they broke the rules. He prided himself on regulation-short hair and a pristine uniform. Inferno Force warriors let their hair grow long and sported tight shirts that showed off plenty of ink. Still, he knew he should be grateful to be on the mission with them.

The rough Drexian warriors rarely let others join them on missions. They preferred to operate on the outskirts of the galaxy, out of reach of the Drexian High Command. Commanders and captains of Inferno Force ran their fleets and ships with a fight hard, play hard mentality. It was a sharp contrast to the protocol expected from officers on the Boat, but one Kos was glad to adapt to since he'd had to fight for the right to join them.

Kos thought back to the meeting where the rescue mission had been finalized and to his own out-of-character behavior. He'd finally been allowed to join the Inferno Force mission only because one of the missing human women was the tribute bride assigned to him, and he'd argued vehemently that it was his duty to hunt for her. His face warmed as he remembered brandishing a blade and threatening harm to anyone who tried to keep him off the mission. The Inferno Force captain leading the mission had liked his insubordination. Any warrior with that much passion was welcome on his crew, he'd said once Kos had stopped yelling. Kos did feel passionate about finding his tribute bride. Even though he'd never met her. Especially because he'd never met her.

While he'd been stuck on the station's bridge during the Kronock attack, his tribute bride, Hope, had been meeting with her wedding planner and liaison and learning all about the Drexians and the secret treaty with Earth and how the Boat had been designed specifically to help Drexian warriors woo their new brides and to assist the humans in planning their dream weddings. He'd missed his introduction to her when the station had begun evacuation procedures, and he'd been further delayed when the shuttle he'd been on had crashed onto a jungle planet along with Captain Varden, one of the reject tributes, and the Perogling.

His only comfort had been knowing that his intended bride had been safely evacuated by her wedding planner and liaison, along with a few other human tributes. He knew enough about the Gatazoid wedding planner, Serge, and the Vexling liaison, Reina, to know that they would take good care of the tributes. Of course, that was before he'd discovered that the shuttle with the handlers and tributes had disappeared en route to the Drexian rendezvous outpost where all the residents of the Boat had gone during the Kronock attack.

You should have been with her, he told himself for the hundredth time. His stomach had been a hard ball of fear and regret since he'd found out that Hope was missing. Even though he'd never met the female, he knew she'd been his to protect, and he'd failed.

Just like you failed before, a little voice in the back of his head whispered. He shook it off, but the cold ball in his gut tightened. He would not fail this time. No matter what.

3

"Approaching the last known coordinates of the shuttle," Kalex said, tapping his fingers to slow their speed.

The ship came out of warp and the streaks of light became pinpoints again, flickering in the inky space around them.

Kos stepped forward, scanning the emptiness. "They're gone now. Any residual power signatures we can track?"

More tapping on the console. "Nothing from our shuttle, but then again, we do have the most sophisticated shielding technology in the galaxy. There is a faint trace of something, but..."

"Why are we slowing?" Brok, the Inferno Force captain leading the mission, strode onto the bridge, his heavy boots announcing his arrival along with his loud voice. Like all Drexians, he was big and bulky, but he seemed to be more tattooed and more scarred than most. Even for an Inferno Force warrior. He wore his dark hair long, although there was nothing remotely feminine about it. A scar slashed through one eyebrow, but that only served to draw more attention to his aquamarine blue eyes.

"We've reached the last known location of the vessel," his first officer said without turning.

Brok grunted, nodding at Kos, his mouth quirking up slightly. "Glad to see you lost the uniform jacket, Officer."

Kos shifted. "Yes, sir."

He'd taken off his Drexian military jacket after he'd realized that no one on the Inferno Force crew wore them—and after the captain had told him to. Even though it felt odd to be in only a black T-shirt and cargo pants on the bridge of a ship, he had to admit it was more comfortable.

"Anything out there?" Brok asked, turning his attention back to his pilot.

"I was just telling Kos that I'm picking up on something," Kalex said, his fingers flying across the shiny black console. "It's a power signature we haven't seen in a long time."

Brok folded his arms over his chest. "Tell me that's a good thing."

Kalex spun around. "Only if you think Ganthar pirates are good."

"Grek." The captain spat out the word, his face darkening.

"Ganthar pirates?" Kos asked, looking from the pilot to the captain. "I thought they'd all but disappeared in our sector."

"Apparently not," Kalex muttered as he turned back to his console.

Kos drew in a breath, trying not to think about what this might mean for Hope and all the abducted females. "Okay, so we go after these pirates."

"I can track their signature," Kalex said. "I don't know how much of a lead they have on us, but we'll hunt them down."

Brok nodded. "Send a transmission to our sister ship. We'll need them to rendezvous. Ganthar pirates aren't something we mess around with."

"They can't be any match for Drexian technology or Inferno Force," Kos said.

"They aren't," the captain said, "but they also aren't constrained by honor or fair fighting. We've been ambushed by Ganthar pirates before. They aren't to be trusted."

Kos swallowed hard. His bride was potentially being held by pirates with no honor. Even though he didn't know her, he felt sick at the thought of one of the small, feminine humans being held at the mercy of space pirates. He'd seen images of Hope—her long blonde hair, her warm brown eyes. His chest swelled at the thought of holding her in his arms and telling her how sorry he was.

Sorry for not meeting her earlier. Sorry for not being with her during the evacuation. Sorry for not preventing her ship from being intercepted.

Brok clapped a thick hand on Kos's shoulder. "We will get her back. We will get all of them back."

Kos nodded. Inferno Force never doubted their abilities. He knew that came from years of fighting off the Kronock. Even though their enemy had recently revealed previously unknown technology, and had landed a few considerable blows to Drexian forces, Inferno Force was no less sure that they would beat them back.

Kos wished he had the same bold confidence as these warriors. His success had always come from working harder than everyone else, nothing more. He'd become the first officer of the Boat by putting in long hours, not by just knowing he could do it. That kind of confidence seemed to be relegated to warriors like those on Inferno Force.

But he *had* become first officer, he reminded himself. The officer that Captain Varden trusted above all others. The officer who would put the job above everything else and never let his superiors down.

Which is why you didn't meet your bride, the nagging voice said. *You were too busy on the bridge. She was evacuated without you while you got Captain Varden off.*

Kos squeezed his hands into fists. He had never imagined she would be taken. How could he have? It was unthinkable.

"Setting a new course," Kalex said, moments before the ship jumped to warp speed again.

"Ready to battle some pirates?" Brok asked him.

Kos squared his shoulders and met the captain's gaze. "Ready, sir."

"Good." Brok propelled him off the bridge. "Now let's go make you look like you're ready."

CHAPTER
TWO

Hope paced a tight circle in her cell, spinning on her heel each time she reached the steel bench that ran along the back wall. She'd coiled her long blonde hair up into a topknot, but it kept coming loose and falling back down.

"You really should try to relax, hon," the blue-haired woman named Reina said from where she sat on the bench, her long legs crossed at the knees and her top leg jiggling up and down.

Hope paused to take in the alien for a moment, wondering how the creature could sound so calm when she was clearly just as nervous as her. "How am I supposed to relax? I was abducted from Earth and taken to a space station where I was told I'd been picked to be a tribute bride for a Drexian warrior—whatever that is—and before I could even absorb all that ridiculousness, we were evacuating the supposed space station because we were being attacked by other aliens and then our ship was intercepted and I was knocked unconscious. When I finally woke up, you tell me that we've been taken captive by Ganthar pirates. That was a few days ago, and we're still stuck in this cell with no idea where we're going or what's going to happen to us. Did I leave anything out?"

Reina gave a nervous laugh. "No. I think that about covers it, but you forgot that the Drexians will be coming after us."

"Right." Hope snapped her fingers. "The mythical Drexian warriors who are, according to you, the biggest badasses in the galaxy."

"They are," Reina said, her gray face earnest as she bobbed her head up and down. "I know you were too overwhelmed to notice them much on the Boat, but they're quite impressive. And I have no doubt they're searching for us right now. I'm sure your groom is sick with worry."

Hope put her hands on her hips. "My groom? That's a phrase I never thought I'd hear. If there's a Drexian warrior that I'm matched with—or so you claim—then why didn't I meet him earlier? Was he not on the space station?"

Reina nibbled her lower lip. "Actually, he was, but..."

"But he was as wild about the idea of marrying a stranger as I was?" Hope resumed her pacing and whipped her loose hair up into a knot again.

"Oh, no. That's not it. I'm sure he was very pleased to be matched with you," Reina said. "But Kos is the first officer of the space station, so I'm sure he was incredibly busy when we had to evacuate. It had nothing to do with you."

Hope raised an eyebrow. "Nothing to do with me? How flattering."

Reina smiled. "I'm glad you think so."

So much for aliens getting sarcasm, Hope thought. It hadn't been bad being stuck in the cell with the tall alien who claimed to be a Vexling. At least she'd had someone to talk to, but the nervous creature definitely didn't get her sense of humor.

"So, we just have to hope that these Drexians get here before what...? The Ganthar pirates make us walk the space plank?"

Reina's gray skin lost a few shades. "Oh, no. I don't think they would do that." She tapped a bony finger on the side of her face. "I don't even think they have a space plank."

"Kidding," Hope muttered. "What do these wankers do when they take prisoners anyway?"

Reina stood and crossed to the circular door with a small round window, peering out into the dim, gunmetal gray corridor. "I don't know for sure. Usually they steal things they can sell."

Hope gulped. "We're going to be sold? Like as slaves?"

Reina shook her head. "I'm sure we'll be rescued by the Drexians before that happens."

Hope sank onto the metal bench and put her head in her hands. Even though she'd pitched a fit when she'd woken up on the Drexian space station, she wished she was there now. The holographic fantasy suite that had been designed to look, smell, and feel like a Caribbean bungalow seemed like a lifetime away now. Why had she been such a pain in the ass to everyone when she'd found herself overlooking the crystal blue waters? Why had she been horrible to the little wedding planner with purple hair?

Because they'd freaked her out, that was why. You couldn't expect to tell someone they'd been taken off their planet by aliens and conscripted to be a bride and have them go along with it. Her reaction—disbelief followed by hostility and threats followed by hysteria—had been totally normal. At least for her.

Hope had been on her own for so long that the idea of being told what to do by anyone made her bristle. And the idea of her entire future being dictated to her made Hope want to run away screaming. She'd always prided herself on her independence—it's what came from having a space cadet mother who'd eventually run off with her shaman—and no way was she going to be mated to some alien stranger without a fight.

"What happens then?" She looked up at Reina. "What happens when we're rescued?"

Reina's expression brightened. "Then we go back to the Boat, or if the station was damaged too much, to the rendezvous outpost."

"So, no chance I'll be taken back to Earth?"

"Once a human is taken to be a tribute bride, they can't be

returned to Earth," Reina said. "Can you imagine the hysteria if women went back and started talking about aliens and space stations and invasions?"

The Vexling had a point. It would create pandemonium.

"What if I promised not to talk?"

Reina smiled at her, her wide eyes unblinking. "Of course, I would believe you, hon, but it's not up to me. I'm just a liaison. I don't make the rules."

Hope nodded. It probably didn't make sense to worry about the Drexians taking her back to Earth when she hadn't even been rescued yet. Reina seemed convinced it was inevitable, but they'd already been held captive for several days. Hope didn't want to think about the other alternative—being sold into alien slavery. Being a tribute bride didn't sound so bad in comparison.

Reina walked over and sat next to her on the bench. "Just you wait until you meet some of the other brides. You'll love them. There are women from all over. Even a couple from New Zeenland, like you."

"New Zealand," Hope corrected. "There are really other Kiwis on the station?"

Reina nodded. "Not a lot, but there are some. Tribute brides come from all over. I know you'll make some good friends once you get to know them."

Hope returned Reina's eager smile. She wasn't so sure about that. Making friends had never been one of her strengths. It was why she'd spent the past few years traveling around the world as a travel blogger. She preferred to be on the move, meeting new people all the time, but never stopping to get too attached to anyone.

It was the same philosophy she had for men. Meet a bunch, have fun, move on. No one got attached. No one got hurt.

"Maybe," she said, trying not to make any promises she couldn't keep.

Reina patted her hand, opening her mouth to say something as the door to their cell swung back.

Both women jumped to their feet. No one had come in since they'd been pushed inside days ago. Meals had been passed through a slat at the bottom of the door and no one had responded to her pounding.

The tall, bulky alien who stepped inside carried a large weapon of some kind, his gaze raking over both of them. It settled on Reina. "You're a Vexling?"

Reina worked her hands together, letting out a small squeak in response.

The alien pirate with dark dreadlocks jerked his head. "Come with me."

Reina looked at Hope. "I can't leave my tribute. You see, I'm a liaison for the tribute brides and I can't leave her alone—"

"Now!" The yell made both Hope and Reina jump as he lifted the hefty weapon onto his shoulder and aimed it at Hope. "Unless you want me to eliminate your reason for staying behind."

Hope grabbed Reina's hand and squeezed it. "It's okay. I'll be fine." She didn't believe a word she was saying, but she needed the Vexling to go without either of them getting hurt.

Reina's lips became a thin white line, but she nodded. "Don't worry. I'm sure they just want to talk to me. I'll be back before you know it." She squeezed Hope's hand back. "Serge is in the cell next to us, and the other brides are across the corridor, so you're not totally alone."

The alien pirate snorted a laugh. "You mean the Gatazoid? We sold him yesterday. His kind fetch a high price on the market."

Reina's hands went limp in hers. "You sold Serge?"

The pirate's lips curled into a sneer. "And the other females. No one had seen humans before, but apparently the small creatures appeal to some." The way he looked at Hope, she knew he did not count himself in that group, which was fine by her. "You're the last one to go, Vexling."

"Go?" Reina's voice was barely audible. "You're selling me?"

"That's right. We've got a buyer looking for a Vexling." He shrugged. "Something about protocol."

Hope instinctively tightened her grip on Reina's hand. "You can't just sell people like this."

He laughed and his belly shook. "Beg your pardon, girlie, but we can. Don't worry, though. We're not selling you." He looked her up and down. "The captain likes the look of you."

Hope's mouth went dry. That didn't sound good. When had the captain even seen her? She glanced at the window in the door. Unless he'd been watching her when she didn't know it. She rubbed one arm, the thought making her skin prickle.

"Move it, Vexling," the pirate yelled again. "Before I have to come in and drag you out."

Hope released Reina's hand and gave her a little push, even though what she really wanted to do was jump in front of her to keep her from leaving. "Don't worry. I'll be fine."

Reina's wide eyes glistened with tears, and Hope forced a fake smile onto her face.

"The Drexians are coming for me, right?" she whispered. "Well, when they do, I promise to come find you and get you back."

Reina stumbled forward and let herself be taken out of the cell, her gaze never leaving Hope's face. When the door slammed shut, Hope staggered back and collapsed onto the bench, trying to steady her ragged breathing and keep herself from crying.

She may not have known Reina well or for long, but the blue-haired woman had been kind to her. And they had been in the mess together.

Now she was alone. Again.

CHAPTER

THREE

Kos swiped at his damp brow. "More."

Captain Brok stepped back, readjusting the long curved blades in his hands. "You're not bad. You ever consider Inferno Force?"

They'd been sparring in the bare-bones ring for a while and both Drexians shone with sweat. Although the Inferno Force captain was skilled, Kos was faster.

Kos shook his head. "Weapons were never my strong suit."

The captain cocked his head to one side. "I'm not so sure about that. You've been out-maneuvering me this entire time."

"That's because of my practice on the Boat's holodecks," Kos said, sucking in a breath. "I like to keep up my practice with the traditional Drexian blades."

Brok slashed at him again. "Not many officers do that. Most are content with blasters once they finish the Drexian Academy."

"Blasters do not help when you are fighting a Kranji master. Even a holographic one is deadly." Kos feinted to one side. He did not say what he wanted to—that he could not be most officers. He had to work harder and be better. He had to prove himself to be

13

worthy. And that meant doing things other officers did not. Like grueling Kranji practice every day after his shift.

"Kranji? That explains it then. Who introduced you to the alien martial art?"

"My captain on the Boat."

Brok dragged the back of his hand across his slick brow. "I heard that about Varden. He is a master, no?"

"He is." Kos did not say that his skills were coming close to equaling those of his mentor.

"You aspire to be captain of the Boat one day?" Brok asked, ducking Kos's lunge.

Kos had never thought about taking Varden's place. The work, and receiving recognition for his achievements, had always been the goal. When he thought about filling Captain Varden's shoes, he twitched.

"No?" Brok heaved in a breath.

"Captain is a huge honor," Kos said.

"I know it is, but you must have thought about it."

Had he? Or had he been so focused on his work that the advancements had passed by in a blur? He couldn't imagine ever matching up to the honor and valor of his captain. Or of this Inferno Force captain.

"I suspect you underestimate yourself," Brok said, moving around the edge of the ring. "Just as you now underestimate your ability to beat me."

Kos didn't answer.

"The only difference between Inferno Force and the rest of the Drexian fleet is that we never believe we will be defeated. Ever. We go into every battle assuming we will win. Not just prevail but win decisively. We know without a shadow of a doubt that we will crush everyone in our path. Always."

"And do you?" Kos asked, adjusting his grip on the curved blades in his hands.

Brok gave him a half grin. "Always." He spun and lashed out again, but Kos blocked him, dipping low and kicking out a leg.

Brok dodged, but quickly spun and attacked. Kos sidestepped just as swiftly, pivoting and flipping over the captain so that he came up under him with his blade extended.

The Inferno Force captain let out a loud bark of laughter. "I may have to steal you away from Varden's bridge whether you like it or not." He stepped back as Kos stood. "I haven't had a sparring partner as creative as this in years. Most of my warriors rely on their brute strength and aggression. You use strategy and cunning to your advantage." He nodded, looking Kos up and down. "It's easy to see why you're first officer."

Pleasure flushed Kos's cheeks. "Thank you, sir."

"All we need to do is give you some of my team's brazen confidence and there will be no one you cannot defeat."

It was an honor to be commended by the Inferno Force captain but doubt still lingered in the back of Kos's mind. Doubt that he was good enough. Doubt that he deserved what he'd worked for. Doubt that he even deserved a tribute bride. He'd failed once before, when it mattered most, and he'd been chasing redemption that never came ever since.

Memories flooded him—unwanted memories—and the sweat cooled on his body as cold chills went through him, make him shiver violently. He just needed to work harder, be better. He gave himself a shake and adjusted the grip on his blade.

Brok cocked his head at him. "You okay, warrior?"

Before Kos could assure the man he was, static filled the room.

"Captain." The voice over the comms system drowned out the sound of their heavy breathing.

"Yes?" Brok lowered his blades and dropped his fighting stance.

"We have the Ganthar pirates on our sensors," the warrior's voice continued. "We'll be on top of them soon."

"Understood." Brok hooked his blades back on the wall and motioned for Kos to do the same. "We're on our way."

As they walked through the ship, Kos ran a hand through his choppy brown hair. "I should get my uniform, sir."

"Negative," Brok said. "We don't want you looking like the first officer of a pleasure ship. We want you looking like a Drexian warrior who's ready to rip some space pirates limb from limb for taking his tribute."

Kos's chest swelled, the adrenaline from fighting the Inferno Force captain still surging through his veins. He clenched his fists. He *did* want to make the Ganthar pay for taking his female.

Brok cut his eyes to him, and one side of his mouth twitched up. "Just like that."

When they reached the compact bridge, Kalex had an image of the pirate ship on the view screen. The ship was long with two segments connected by a disc-shaped center. It did not look like a ship built for speed or battle, but Kos knew looks could be deceiving.

"Weapons?" Brok asked, leaning his hands against the back of an empty swivel chair.

"Moderate. Nothing we can't handle," Kalex said. "And our other Inferno Force ships are right behind us, so the Ganthar are about to be seriously outmatched."

Brok nodded. "We've dealt with them before, though. They could very well be hiding another ship or two nearby."

"No moons or other planetary bodies to hide behind here. Unless they've developed stealth technology since our last encounter, we'll see them coming."

"What's the strategy?" Kos asked, folding his arms across his chest, his muscles still tingling from the workout.

Kalex glanced at him, his eyebrows popping up when he saw the Drexian shirtless and gleaming with sweat. "Looks like we'll make an Inferno Force warrior out of you yet." When the captain tapped his toe on the floor, he cleared his throat and continued. "The plan is to threaten to blow them out of the sky unless they turn over our people."

Captain Brok glared at the image of the pirate ship. "Which is not a threat."

Kos flinched. "My tribute bride is most likely on that ship. We should negotiate for their release. The pirates aren't stupid. They'll know the humans are valuable to us."

"You are right," the captain said. "They've got something we want. We need to go on board and take it."

The console beeped, and Kalex looked down. "They're hailing us."

Brok exchanged a glance with Kos. "On screen."

Kalex tapped the console, and the view screen filled with the image of a wild-haired alien with dark skin. He was flanked by several menacing figures.

"Inferno Force," the pirate captain said. "What an unexpected pleasure."

Brok braced his hands on his waist, flexing the muscles of his broad, bare chest. "You have some things that belong to us."

The pirate tilted his head and gave a cold smile. "Do I?"

"We are prepared to come on board and negotiate for their release," Brok said.

"Our sister ship just jumped in," Kalex said low enough so only Brok and Kos could hear.

It was clear from the flicker on the Ganthar pirate's face that he was aware of the second Inferno Force ship's arrival. "We welcome you on board to look at what we have for sale."

Kos tried to keep his face impassive even as he felt his arms twitch. He wanted to reach through the screen and rip the pirate's smug smile off his face.

"Expect our arrival," the captain said, slashing a hand, indicating that Kalex should end the connection. When the screen returned to the view of the ship, Brok put a hand on his pilot's shoulder. "We'll take the shuttle. Keep weapons locked on until we're clear. And keep communications open."

Kalex gave a curt nod.

The Inferno Force captain turned to Kos. "Let's go get your tribute."

CHAPTER
FOUR

"Where are you taking me?" Hope jerked against the tight grip of the pirate as he practically dragged her out of her cell. Even though she hadn't been crazy about being locked inside, she knew that being taken out meant that she was being sold. Or worse.

"The captain requests your presence."

Okay, that was worse than being sold. She had no intention of being the pirate captain's booty call or concubine or anything like that. "If you think I'm going to…"

Her words died in her throat as she entered a large circular space with a metal chair at the far end. A man with a mane of black hair sat in it, his hands gripping the arms and his gaze locked onto her. Other men stood behind him, and from what she could see, they were the definition of a rag-tag bunch. They wore no uniforms, and most of them looked like they'd scavenged their clothes. Only the leader looked as if he hadn't taken his clothes from a rubbish bin, his brown pants and shirt topped with a heavy fur cloak.

"Welcome, my dear," he said, his voice artificially pleasant. He waved her forward. "We are expecting some guests who are very eager to see you."

Hope allowed herself to be prodded forward until she stood in front of the captain. He looked her up and down and smiled coolly. "I've heard of the humans the Drexians obtain for mating purposes, but you and your friends are the first ones I've seen for myself."

She held her head high even though her hands shook by her sides. She would not let them see how scared she was.

The captain shrugged. "I can see the appeal, although I cannot speak from personal experience." He leered at her. "Yet."

Hope swallowed the bitter taste of bile that threatened to rise up in her throat. *Play it cool,* she told herself. *Do not throw up all over him.*

"Yeah, that's never going to happen," she said, with as much disdain as she could muster.

The captain's eyes flashed for a moment, then he threw his head back and laughed. "You have spirit, I'll give you that." He leaned forward, smiling with a mouthful of teeth as brown as his skin. "A spirit I might enjoy breaking."

Hope refused to look away, although his leering grin made her heart pound even harder. It took every ounce of self-control—and that wasn't something she was known for—not to make a run for it. "Thanks for the offer, but I think I'll pass."

The captain's grin faltered. "We'll see about that."

She swallowed hard but didn't drop her eyes. She would not let him see that her hands were trembling or that the blood was pulsing so loud in her ears she felt lightheaded.

All the crew tensed as heavy footsteps echoed in the corridor. The pirate who'd brought her from her cell pulled her to the side, positioning her behind the captain. Hope let out a breath, relieved not to be facing off with the captain anymore, although the way the crew was reacting, she wasn't sure if what was approaching would be any better for her.

Whoever was coming to look at her had to be pretty important and pretty scary for these tough pirates to be so tense. When the two aliens entered the space, she had to admit she was startled.

She'd expected some sort of shocking giants, or an impressive group of terrifying creatures, or a massive fleet of soldiers with huge guns, but it was only a pair of shirtless guys with blades and blasters hooked to their belts. They were big, she'd give them that, and both were seriously built, with bulging biceps and massive chest muscles. One had longer hair and tattoos across his chest and arms, while the other had brown hair cut short.

It was the one with short hair who made her catch her breath. His gray eyes held hers from across the room, and she felt her chest lurch. Why did she feel like she'd met him before? The way he stared at her, he definitely thought he knew her. Had she met him on the space station?

Her time on the Boat was a bit of a blur. She'd spent most of it pitching a fit and refusing to believe that she'd been abducted by aliens. It was very possible she'd met the guy and didn't remember, although she liked to think she'd remember someone as hot as him. No, most of her interactions on the fancy space station had been with other tribute brides or funny-looking aliens like Reina and Serge. Plus, the guys on the station had all been in stiff, dark uniforms, not shirtless and wild-looking like the two aliens in front of her now.

You're imagining things, she told herself. *You would definitely remember a gorgeous guy like him if you were introduced to him on the Boat, and where else would you meet someone out in space?*

She tried to pull her gaze from his, but couldn't, and had to remind herself to breathe.

The pirate captain swiveled his head to look at her, his head tilting in curiosity. "It looks like no introductions are needed, although I think I should be jealous. Our remaining female guest has never looked at me like this before." He grabbed her hand and jerked her forward, then slapped her ass. "Who is this warrior to you?"

Hope struggled in his grip. "Get your fucking hands off me, you wanker."

The pirate captain grinned widely but tugged her closer, and Hope noticed the warrior who'd been staring at her flinch, his expression darkening. She tried to steady her breathing, and she saw that the heavily tattooed man shot the other a look of warning before stepping forward.

"We are here to negotiate the release of the human captives."

The pirate captain leaned back in his huge chair, pulling Hope so that she was forced to sit on his lap. "There is only the one. I am open to selling her, although I must admit she intrigues me. If you do not offer a good price, I might be tempted to keep her for my own amusement."

"Not in a million fucking years," Hope said, shooting daggers at the captain.

He grabbed her jaw quickly, squeezing it until she drew in a sharp breath from the pain. "I would be careful if I were you, female."

The man who'd been staring at her let out a low rumble that reverberated against the curved metal walls.

The other warrior ignored it but shifted one hand closer to his blade. "We do not take kindly to our brides being damaged. Where are the others?"

"Sold." The captain dropped Hope's chin and waved his hand in the air. "You do understand the concept of piracy, don't you?"

His men laughed behind him, and both of the visiting men tensed.

The tattooed man shrugged. "Of course. Just as you, no doubt, understand the concept of Inferno Force warships."

The pirate captain let out a weary breath. "You Drexians always make everything a battle."

Drexians? These were Drexians? Hope squinted at the two men. She'd seen some of the Drexians when she'd been evacuated off the Boat, but she'd been too irritated and freaked out to pay much attention to them. At the time, she thought they looked like over-sized human men in military uniforms.

Well, these guys were certainly big, but they'd lost the uniforms. And aside from being big, they didn't look very much like aliens. Or, she should say, what she'd thought aliens would look like. Their skin was bronze, and they appeared to have no bonus appendages. Even Serge and Reina had looked more alieny than the Drexians.

"We do not wish for a battle," the tattooed Drexian said. "But we are always prepared to fight to the death."

"Yes." The pirate captain rapped his fingers on the arm of his chair. "That's one thing we can count on."

Tattoo shrugged. "We'd hate to disappoint."

The pirate captain leaned forward, a grin creasing his face. "I have a proposition for you, Drexian warriors."

Both Drexians shifted slightly, as if bracing.

"I will give you the human." He ran a rough hand through Hope's hair without looking at her. "But only if you entertain me. I've always wanted to see a Drexian in action."

No one spoke, and the captain flopped back in his chair, readjusting Hope so she was nestled between his thighs. "Fight one of my men for her, and she's yours."

"Agreed," the Drexian with short hair who hadn't spoken before said, causing the other man to snap his head over to him.

"Not so fast," Tattoo said. "Who does he fight?"

The pirate captain rubbed his hands together, and she was pushed out of the way as the crew parted, revealing a hulking creature with horns curling out of the top of his head.

For a moment, Hope wished the tattooed Drexian had been the one to volunteer to fight for her. On the surface, he looked more menacing. Then she locked eyes with the Drexian who had agreed to the fight. His eyes blazed fury as he pulled out his blade, then he focused his gaze on her and her mouth went dry. She could almost feel his rage pulsing from all the way across the room. Maybe this was the warrior she wanted fighting for her, after all.

CHAPTER
FIVE

Kos drew in a long, steady breath, his gaze on his tribute bride. He'd seen her image before, but only on a view screen, and that hadn't done justice to her. It hadn't been able to portray how her eyes sparkled and how sexy her pale hair looked when it was tousled around her face.

A static image also didn't portray her quick mouth or her fondness for Earth curses. He suspected that if they didn't get her out soon, her sharp responses to the pirate captain would land her in serious trouble, although Kos had to admit feeling a certain amount of pride that she'd snapped back at her captor. His mate was brave, even if she needed to learn to temper her impulses.

He'd quickly assessed that she wasn't hurt. Scared, yes, but he didn't see any bruises or signs of mistreatment. Not that he thought the Ganthar space pirates were humanitarians. He was sure they wanted to maximize their profit when they sold her, and a healthy slave was much more appealing than a battered one.

The pirate leader grinned as his fighter strode forward. He was clearly enjoying this, grinning widely as the horned creature cracked his neck and prepared for battle.

"You don't need to do this," Captain Brok said to him under his breath. "We have enough firepower to take them out."

The Ganthar captain reached back and tugged Hope forward, pulling her back down into his lap as she slapped at him.

"Get your fucking hands off me, you fuckwit."

Kos's skin prickled with heat as he watched Hope struggle while the pirate gave her a swat on the ass and settled her between his legs. "Yes, I do need to do this."

Brok looked from the horned alien to him and sighed. "You're sure you're not secretly Inferno Force?"

Kos gave him a brief smile. "Thanks. Just get the female out of here, whatever happens."

Brok passed him his own blade, which was longer than Kos's. "Take this. And all that ducking and moving you did with me? Do even more of it with this guy."

Kos took the blade and nodded, then turned his attention to his opponent and stepped into the wide open circle on the floor.

The horned pirate was also shirtless, but he had straps criss-crossing his slightly furry chest that were studded with metal. Kos made a mental note to avoid getting in a lock with the guy. Those studs would not feel great jabbed into his flesh.

The creature's eyes were small and solid red, giving him the appearance of a demon, and his horns were nearly black, with sharp points at the ends. Something else to avoid.

Kos's heart knocked in his ribcage, but not from fear. Anger coursed through him, firing his blood and making his fingers tingle in anticipation. He wanted to rip the pirates apart for holding his tribute captive, but even more for frightening her. Seeing Hope fight off the pirate captain as the alien put his hands on her sent fresh waves of rage through him.

The horned pirate sidestepped around the edge of the makeshift ring, his huge feet echoing off the metal floor. He didn't hold any weapons, but he flexed his meaty hands, his knuckles cracking.

Kos knew he should be worried. The alien was clearly comfortable in hand-to-hand combat and was confident enough not to feel the need for weapons, even as Kos stood across from him holding two curved blades. If he'd been thinking straight, Kos might think he was outmatched. But he wasn't thinking. He was reacting to the sight of another male touching his mate. He growled and twisted the blades in his hands.

The pirate crew cheered loudly as the fighters circled each other, but the Inferno Force captain did not move from where he stood on the edge, his thick arms crossed. He didn't seem worried, although Kos had never seen an Inferno Force warrior appear worried. It didn't seem to be in their DNA.

Focusing on his opponent, Kos watched the way he moved. He was big, but he wasn't fast. His steps were deliberate, and when he moved closer and thrust out an arm in a punch, the movement was powerful, but plodding. Kos ducked easily, rolling underneath him and coming up on the other side, spinning and swiping at the pirate's bare arm.

His blade nicked him, and the creature howled. Rushing forward, the alien lowered his head to butt Kos with his curved horns. Kos saw it coming and spun to the side, hitting the pirate hard on the head with the flat of one of his blades. The metal made a loud noise as it hit the horns, and the alien staggered back, shaking his head.

The pirate crew groaned and jeered, their yells angry. Kos glanced over at Hope. Her eyes were fixed on him, and she nibbled the edge of her bottom lip. He wanted to tell her not to worry, but before he could open his mouth or even give her a comforting smile, he saw a flash out of the corner of his eye. The horned alien plowed into him, lifting him off his feet and slamming him onto the ground.

All the air rushed out of Kos, but he managed to roll away before the creature could slam a heavy foot down on his face. He jumped up, slightly dazed, and danced to the other side of the ring. The pirate bore down on him again, but Kos was ready. Feinting to one side, he pivoted quickly then somersaulted in the air and came down behind his opponent, slashing at the creature's hamstrings.

With a bellow of pain, the alien sank to the ground as blood rushed from the backs of his legs. The pirate crew gasped and then went quiet. The captain leapt to his feet, causing Hope to fall forward onto the floor.

"Enough!" the Ganthar leader said, holding up a fist. He stared at his crew member, his lips twisted in disgust. "You've made your point."

Kos was breathing hard, but he straightened and lowered his blades. "We'll take the female now."

The captain grunted, looking down at Hope and kicking her down the few steps to the open area. She yelped, but caught herself with her arms, standing and shooting daggers over her shoulder at the alien.

Kos tossed Brok his blade, and the Inferno Force captain stood over the horned pirate as he lay on the floor grasping his legs and howling.

Kos strode forward, fighting the urge to run, and put an arm around Hope. He searched her face, and she managed to give him a weak smile. "I'm fine."

Brok met his eyes as he walked Hope away from the rumbling pirate crew. "Go to the shuttle. I have unfinished business with our Ganthar friends."

Kos hesitated, twisting his head and seeing the pirate captain flinch.

"You have what you came for," he said, baring his grimy teeth.

"Not quite." Brok flexed his shoulders and readjusted his grip on his blade. "Before we can leave you to continue your life of piracy, I'm going to need the names of who you sold all our humans and crew members to."

The Ganthar leader leaned back, clenching the armrests until his knuckles went white. "You'll never find them all. By now they're spread across the galaxy."

Brok gave the man a smile that made Kos go cold. "For your sake, let's hope that is not the case."

Kos realized that neither he nor Hope was breathing. He tightened his grip around her shoulders and propelled her forward, out of the round chamber of the pirate ship. Hurrying down the steel corridor, her body stiffened as they passed door after door with small porthole windows.

"Are these the cells where they held you?" he asked.

She nodded but didn't speak. When they were halfway down the long, curving hallway, Hope stopped. Her eyes were downcast, and he thought she might feel ill.

"We're almost to the shuttle," he said. "Soon you'll be off this ship forever."

"I don't suppose the shuttle is very big?"

He shook his head. "Not really. The three of us will fit, though."

She bent down and picked up a flat steel card lying on the floor. "They may not be able to come with us, but maybe this will give them a fighting chance." She moved quickly to one of the cells, inserting the card into a slot and standing back as the door swung open.

Kos watched open-mouthed as she moved quickly down the rest of the hallways, opening doors and freeing prisoners. Soon the corridor was filled with aliens of all kinds, many of them clearly fighters bound for gladiator slavery.

When she'd freed everyone, she handed the access card to one of the prisoners. "If I were you, I'd head to the bridge. You should be able to take control of the ship before the crew knows what's going on."

Brok ran up to them, his head swiveling as he took in the aliens moving freely. "What's going on? I thought you two were already in the shuttle."

"Slight detour," Hope said. "Just had to start a revolution before we left."

Brok cut his eyes to Kos. "I like her." He pushed them both

forward toward the waiting shuttle, lowering his voice. "But you're going to have your hands full, my friend."

Kos took Hope by the hand, pulling her behind him and running as screams erupted behind them. So much for a smooth getaway.

He suspected the captain was right about his bride. She was far from a helpless female.

CHAPTER
SIX

Hope rushed onto the shuttle behind the Drexians. Her heart was racing, partly from running and partly from the exhilaration of releasing all the prisoners and unleashing them onto the pirate crew.

"That was awesome," she said, pausing after running up the ramp.

The two Drexians exchanged a look, and the one who'd fought for her pushed her down into a chair and strapped her in before taking one of the black swivel chairs in front of the main console.

"Come on, guys," she said, heaving in a breath as the ramp behind her slammed shut and the engines powered up. "You have to admit that was pretty amazing."

"Let's get out of here," the tattooed Drexian said, tapping the shiny console as the ship shot forward and out of the small hangar bay.

Hope peered out the slanted front window of the ship as they burst into space. Two hulking gray ships hovered nearby, and they appeared to be heading toward the smaller of the two.

"Did the captain give you the names of the buyers?" one of the Drexians asked the other.

The other nodded. "He was right that they're spread out. He didn't sell the brides and our crew members to just one alien. For the most part, he sold them individually. It will take one ship a while to track them all down."

"You should take two."

The tattooed warrior cocked his head. "We need to get your tribute bride back to the outpost first."

Hope made a face. Were they talking about her? "Hey! Do you mean me? Am I the 'tribute' you need to take somewhere?" She held her fingers up to make air quotes.

Both aliens turned to face her.

"First of all," she continued after taking a breath, "I have a name, and it's Hope. Second of all, I'm no one's tribute, and I'm certainly not a bride."

The Drexian who'd fought for her flinched. "My name is Kos of House Kavison and you are, in fact, my tribute bride."

Hope arched an eyebrow at him. "Well, it's nice to meet you, Kos. I appreciate the rescue and all, but, like I said, I'm no one's bride."

The edges of the tattooed Drexian's mouth trembled, and he spun back around. "Regardless, we cannot take her to rescue the rest of the tributes. She must be taken back to the outpost."

"Agreed, Captain Brok," Kos said. "I will take her back in this shuttle. You and the rest of the Inferno Force hunting party should take both ships to find the others."

Brok studied him for a moment. "You are sure you wish to take her back alone?" He slid his eyes to her. "You know tribute brides have been known to be less than cooperative."

Kos also glanced at her, then back at the captain. "We will be fine. Taking an Inferno Force ship from the hunt will lose valuable time. The faster you can go after the tributes and missing crew members, the faster you can get them back."

"Are you talking about going after the other women who were

abducted?" Hope asked. "Because I should go with you. I could help."

"Out of the question," Kos said. "It's too dangerous."

She narrowed her eyes at him. "Because I'm a woman or because I'm human?"

"Both," Captain Brok said. "We cannot risk you again after finding you, and there is no place for a female on an Inferno Force ship."

Hope huffed out a breath and sat back. She hated the idea of being hurried off to safety while the other women—not to mention Serge and Reina—were still out there. She thought about the kind-hearted Vexling, and her throat tightened.

The shuttle approached the smaller of the two ships, sliding into an opening on one end. They hovered above the hangar bay before setting down with a small shudder.

The captain stood, giving her a brief bow. "I wish you a quick journey and a happy bonding."

Hope's mouth opened and closed. That was definitely the strangest goodbye she'd ever gotten. "Uh, thanks, I think."

He pivoted to Kos, who had also stood. The Drexians clasped each other's arms at the elbow.

"There is always a place for a warrior like you in Inferno Force," the captain said. "A fighter like you should not be stuck on a space station bridge."

Kos nodded, something between regret and acceptance flickering across his face. "Thank you, Captain. Good hunting, sir."

Brok released his grip and gave the warrior a flicker of a smile. "Good luck."

He strode off the shuttle, and Kos twisted back around toward the console as the ramp started to rise again.

"That's it?" Hope asked, unhooking her safety straps. "We're leaving?"

Kos glanced over his shoulder. "You should be seated during takeoff."

She took the seat at the console that the captain had abandoned, giving him a sweet smile. "Better?"

He shrugged. "As you wish."

Despite wanting to be angry at him for being so bossy, she couldn't stop her gaze from lingering on his bare chest, still glistening with sweat from his fight and their escape from the ship.

"So, what's the plan?" She tore her gaze from his impressive bare skin and leaned back in the chair. "We fly off into the sunset, get back to this outpost place, get married, and live happily ever after?"

His fingers hesitated over the console. "Something like that."

"One problem, mate. I'm not tribute bride material. I keep telling everyone, but no one listens. I have zero plans to get hitched; I never have. It's not my style to be with one person forever, or even for longer than a month. So, I hate to ruin the plan, but you and I aren't going to happen."

"Then why did you just call me mate?"

"What? I didn't—" She paused and laughed. "Oh, that's an expression. It means friend, not mate the way you think of the word. I call a lot of people 'mate.'"

He frowned as he looked at her, his gray eyes holding hers. Her breath caught in her throat, and she tried to swallow but couldn't. Something flickered in his eyes—some flash of pain—but it vanished quickly, replaced by a smoldering heat that made her suck in her breath. "You are mine, and you know it as well as I do."

She finally found her voice. "Arrogant much?"

"I am not arrogant." He turned back to the controls as the shuttle shot out of the mouth of the hangar bay. "I am only saying what we both know. You will be mine."

The only reason Hope didn't kick the guy in the balls was that he'd fought for her on the pirate ship and kicked some serious ass to get her out of there. That counted for something, but it didn't mean he owned her.

"Listen, I appreciate the hero thing, and I'm glad to be off that pirate ship, but you can't just go around saying that two people who've never met have to get married and spend the rest of their lives together. It's crazy. We don't even know each other."

"I know you are beautiful and brave, and I would give my life to keep you safe."

Hope felt some of the fight leave her. Who talked like that? No guys she'd ever met, although, to be fair, guys who bummed around for a living like her usually weren't the best boyfriend or husband material.

She cleared her throat. "Thanks, but that still doesn't mean I'm going to agree to marry you."

The shuttle banked to one side, arching around the side of the larger ship and flying in the other direction. Kos's fingers danced across the console, his attention seemingly focused on flying, although a vein pulsed in the side of his neck.

"You do not have to," he said. "You can always become one of the rejects."

"Rejects?" She didn't like the sound of that. "What are rejects?"

"Females who reject their matches and reject the tribute bride concept entirely. There is a special part of the station for these females."

She crossed her arms over her chest. "Let me guess. No Caribbean fantasy suites on the reject side?"

He gave a curt shake of his head. "No, but you are welcome to go there if you choose not to accept me."

Irritation made her tap her feet on the floor. "So, let me get this straight. You guys kidnap women, force them to marry total strangers, and if they don't, they get kicked off into the low-rent district?"

"Like I said, it is your choice." He stood, his bare, heavily muscled chest coming within inches of her face as he did. "I do not want an unwilling bride."

Hope's cheeks warmed as her eyes lingered on his hard body. No way did she ever plan to get married, but she wouldn't exactly use the word unwilling to describe her feelings. Her gaze dropped to the bulge in his pants that was currently at eye level. Not about everything, at least.

CHAPTER

SEVEN

K os wanted to hit something. He stood, feeling her eyes on him as he moved to the back of the shuttle. She was infuriating, and he didn't know whether he wanted to spank her or fuck her. Maybe both.

The human female was not at all what he'd expected. She looked pretty and soft, but she was actually difficult and stubborn. Exactly what he *didn't* need in his life. Unfortunately, she also stirred something deep within him, and she made his cock do more than stir. It throbbed every time he looked at her, and he readjusted the hard bulge as it strained uncomfortably in his pants.

Kos pressed one of the panels over his head to reveal a hidden cabinet, and he pawed through the contents until he found a standard-issue shirt. He pulled it over his head, and the black fabric clung to his muscles. A little tight, but wearable.

He glanced back at her, pressing his lips together. Not only was Hope barely grateful for being rescued, but she seemed to have no intention to take a mate. He knew that some tributes took time to warm up to the idea, but he'd expected her to be more receptive once they'd met. Especially after the connection they'd had on the Ganthar ship.

At least, he'd thought they'd had a connection. He knew he'd felt all his blood rush south the moment he'd laid eyes on her. And that lust had morphed into a rage that had fueled his battle the moment he'd seen the pirate captain touch her. He shook his head as he thought back to the murderous fury that had come over him. It wasn't a feeling he'd experienced before, and the lack of control scared him. Was that what Inferno Force warriors felt all the time?

Despite his instinct to protect her with his life, he should have known she was going to be a challenge the second she'd started setting prisoners free. Although he admired the sentiment, it was impulsive and rash. He'd spent most of his life working hard and avoiding doing things that were impulsive. It was why he'd chosen a path of steady advancement on the crew of the Boat instead of risking everything for glory in Inferno Force.

Hope should be with an Inferno Force warrior, he thought. They were equally rash. But then he balled his hands into fists. No, the image of her with one of the rough, tattooed Drexians made him want to hit something even more.

It didn't matter what he thought or what he wanted. Hope was matched to him. She was his. He would kill to keep her by his side and safe. Even if she didn't want him and chose to join the other reject brides, it was his duty to get her back to the rendezvous outpost safely. And Kos never neglected his duty, no matter how painful.

Taking a deep breath to steady himself, he strode back to the pilot's chair. "It will take us a few days to get back to the Drexian outpost, even at warp. If we use jump technology, it would drain the power and leave us dead in the water before we made it."

"Jump technology?"

It was nice talking to her without arguing, and it was a good reminder that his people and their culture were still relatively new to her. He glanced over, and a breath hitched in his throat when he saw her peering up at him from under long lashes. Her brown eyes were warm with flecks of gold and green. He looked away quickly. If he wasn't careful, he could lose himself in them.

"Drexians use jump technology to move ships long distances," he explained, keeping his gaze firmly on the readouts in front of him. "It is an effective strategy to get away from enemies quickly, but it takes a special jump drive, which not all ships have, and it depletes the ship's power reserves. After one or maybe two jumps, a ship will be out of power."

"Someone knows a lot about ships."

"I have to," he said. "Not only am I a Drexian warrior, but I'm first officer of our space station."

"You seem pretty young for that." Hope eyed him. "Were you always an overachiever?"

"I've always had a lot to make up for," he said before he thought better of it.

She swiveled to face him. "What does that mean? Were you a juvenile delinquent as a kid or something?" She held up both palms. "I mean, no judgment. I was supposed to have been a handful."

Memories rushed over him. Memories that made his gut churn and his heart race. He shook his head, as if that would rid him of them. "I'm the only son. I had to achieve."

"I'm an only child, too. Sucks sometimes, doesn't it?"

Kos swallowed a hard lump in his throat. "I was not always an only child. My younger brother died when we were both young."

The cockpit went silent, and Hope touched a hand to his arm. "I'm really sorry."

"I should have saved him. I was older. It was my job to protect him." He closed his eyes briefly, the horrible image flashing through his mind of the ground in front of him exploding and his brother disappearing with it.

"I'm sure it's not your fault. You were just a kid."

He gave another hard shake of his head. "You don't understand."

"You're right," she said, after a moment. "I don't know what that must have been like."

"It doesn't matter." Kos let out a breath, his shoulders uncoiling as he pushed away the feelings of regret and failure. "You were asking about our journey and the ship."

Hope twisted her chair around to face forward. "Well, it's all over my head. I wasn't into science in school, and since then I've been a travel blogger. Not much tech in my job unless you consider my laptop and smart phone."

Kos did not know what either of those things were. "When you are a warrior race tasked with protecting the galaxy, you need to develop technology to keep you one step ahead of your enemies."

"Who are your enemies again?"

He steadied his breathing, as he thought about the aliens who were the reason his brother was dead. "We have been battling the Kronock for generations."

"I think Reina mentioned them in my orientation on the space station," Hope said. "But I might have been yelling a lot at the time."

Kos shook his head. Why did that not surprise him? "They are a despicable race, known for invading other planets and harvesting them for resources."

"Wait. I remember this. They're the ones who want to invade Earth. You guys protect us from them, right?"

"Right." He almost smiled at how proud she seemed of herself for remembering this information. "We protect Earth in exchange for a select number of human females."

"And we're back to the kidnapping part," she mumbled.

"We do not kidnap."

"Are you going to let me go?" she asked.

He hesitated. Even if she did not accept the match with him, she would not be returned to Earth. "Well, no."

"Sounds like kidnapping to me." She stared at him. "What I don't get is why you guys bother with the secrecy thing. I mean, look at you. All you Drexians are gorgeous and built. Most women I know would claw each other's eyes out to get a chance to marry someone like you. If you were upfront about it, you'd have women lining up in the streets."

"But not you?"

She looked away from him. "It's nothing personal, mate. It's like I said before. I'm not a long-term type of girl. I'm more of a love-'em -and-leave-'em type. Emphasis on the leave."

His gut clenched. Despite what she said, her rejection did feel personal. Even if he could admit that she might be too stubborn and too difficult and too everything for him, he still felt that she was his. Clearly, she did not.

He jerked his head behind him. "The journey will be long. You should sleep."

She looked behind her. "Am I supposed to bunk on the floor? Or is there an invisible bed I don't know about?"

He gave her a look, and she shrugged. "What? I don't know how advanced your alien tech is. You could have invisible beds. Wonder Woman had an invisible jet."

He did not know who this Wonder Woman was, and he did not ask. Human culture was confusing to him. He knew the space station had been designed by taking inspiration from Earth culture. It was even called the Boat—short for the Love Boat—after a show about a ship that bobbed about in the water and helped people fall in love. It made no sense.

Standing, Kos walked to the middle of the shuttle and pressed another inset black panel. A bed lowered from the wall, dark sheets tucked around a mattress and a thin pillow expanding on one end.

Hope scanned the rest of the compact space. "What else do you guys have hidden in the walls?"

"Supplies." He gestured behind her. "Another bed."

Her pupils flared slightly, but he turned back to the cockpit. "Like I said, we have a long journey. You should sleep."

Kos returned to the pilot's chair, hearing her crawl into the bed. He focused on the readouts. He'd been telling the truth. It was a long journey to reach the Drexian outpost. Even longer when you were trapped in a small ship with a female who had no intention of accepting your match.

Kos gritted his teeth. He just needed to complete the mission and get her to safety. Then she could join the other reject humans and he could return to work and begin the hard job of forgetting about her.

CHAPTER
EIGHT

Hope lay on the pop-down bed, looking up at the black ceiling of the shuttlecraft. She wasn't tired, but she definitely got the idea that Kos wanted her out of his sight for a while.

Not that she totally blamed him. She *had* told the guy that she had no interest in being his mate, even after he'd flown halfway across the galaxy to find her and fought a horny alien to get her back from the space pirates. She thought back to watching him battle the other alien, and her pulse fluttered.

She wasn't into fights, but even she had to admit that it had been hot to watch Kos battling it out all shirtless and sweaty. She peeked at the Drexian sitting at the ship's controls. He'd put on a shirt, but even now it strained over his considerable muscles. Thinking of those muscles and wondering what they would feel like made her heart stutter in her chest.

What are you doing? Hope turned her gaze back to the ceiling. *You've already made it really clear you want nothing to do with being the guy's match.*

That was true. She didn't want to be his mate or whatever the aliens called it. She didn't want to ever be anyone's wife. She cringed at the thought of being a wifey. No way. That type of commitment wasn't for her.

That didn't mean she couldn't appreciate how hot the alien warrior was. And if she was being honest, he was exactly her type—dark hair, tall, muscular build. The intriguing gray eyes were just icing on the cake. And the cherry on top of that icing was the significant bulge she'd noticed in his pants.

But it was either all or nothing with the Drexians. Either you married the guy they picked for you or it was off to the slums with you. The fact that she couldn't go home to Earth ticked her off.

She remembered Reina telling her how they picked the women they took. Only women with few to no family or friends. It had stung when she'd heard that, and it hurt even more to realize that they'd been right about her. She wasn't super close to anyone. Traveling around for a living hadn't lent itself to tight relationships, not that she'd been looking for that. She'd always preferred moving on before people got tired of her. It was what her mother had done—move on without her—and as much as she'd hated her for it, she couldn't help repeating the pattern. Somehow, it felt safer never getting too close to anyone.

Of course, that hadn't worked out so well, considering she'd been targeted for alien abduction.

If only she could get back to Earth. All she wanted was to return to her old life of traveling the world. She missed the freedom and the adventure. The thought of living on an alien space station forever made her feel like she was being smothered.

Hope took a deep breath. She wouldn't even mention the whole alien abduction thing when she got home. She didn't want everyone to think she was a loon. All she needed was a way to get away from the Drexians and back to Earth.

She swiveled her head around again. Right now, she was only with one Drexian. She'd never have odds this good again, she told herself.

She shook her head. She couldn't do it. Not after everything he'd done for her and after he'd opened up. What kind of bitch attacks the guy who literally risked his life for her and then confessed that he felt responsible for his kid brother dying? The kind of bitch who's desperate to get back to her life, Hope thought.

"I am definitely going to hell for this," she whispered to herself.

Glancing around the shuttle, she saw nothing she could use to incapacitate him. Her eyes lingered on his belt. He still wore a blaster on one side and the curved blade attached to the other. She had no intention of hurting him, but maybe she could knock him out with the hilt of the blade. She didn't trust herself with a blaster.

Getting to the weapon was another matter entirely, though. She'd seen how fast Kos moved. He'd been lightning fast compared to the alien he'd battled, his quick reflexes making his movements almost a blur.

She couldn't just grab for it. He'd see that coming a mile away. She folded her arms on top of the sheet and drummed her fingers on them. She'd have to be more clever and more subtle, and she knew just how to do that.

Even if Kos was an alien—and a badass Drexian warrior, at that —he was still a guy. And she'd never met a guy who wasn't distracted by a little seduction.

Hope knew it wasn't playing fair, but then neither was snatching her off of her planet. Once she was back on Earth, Kos could get another tribute—one who actually wanted to get married. She just hoped he wouldn't add this to the list of things he blamed himself for, because this was not about him. As cheesy as it sounded to say "it's not you, it's me," in this case it was true.

She sat up and slipped her legs out from under the soft sheets, her bare feet touching the hard floor. Her heart was thumping, and she took even breaths to steady it.

Kos swiveled his chair around, raising an eyebrow when he saw she was up. "I thought you were sleeping."

She shrugged, fluttering her eyelashes at him and feeling ridiculous. "Couldn't. I kept thinking about this whole match thing."

"The match you do not want?"

She shimmied her hips as she walked forward. "That's just it, Kos. It's not that I don't want you. It's just the whole forever concept I'm stuck on."

He eyed her warily. "I do not understand."

"Maybe we could try it out and see how we feel afterward," she said, hearing the faint tremor in her voice.

"After what?" The poor guy looked seriously confused, and she felt a pang of guilt.

Hope pushed any regrets out of her mind as she reached him and sat down on top of him, straddling his waist. He inhaled sharply, his gray eyes darkening. She wet her bottom lip. "After this."

She crushed her mouth to his, feeling his shock and then feeling his arms come around her back and pull her tightly into him. His kiss soon became dominant, his hand tangling in her hair as he let out a low growl.

Panic fluttered in her chest as she realized just what type of fire she was playing with.

CHAPTER
NINE

Desire pounded through him as all rational thought fled Kos's mind.

Gods, what was she doing?

He didn't care why she'd started kissing him. He only hoped she wouldn't stop.

Her hair was soft as he wound his fingers through it, pulling her deeper and feeling her lips yield to him. Even though she'd initiated the kiss, she startled when he parted her lips. He tangled his tongue with hers, and she sagged against him, moaning into his mouth and sending fresh waves of need ricocheting through his body.

She tasted just as sweet as she looked, and Kos found himself intoxicated by the feel of her as she writhed in his lap. Slipping his hands from her hair down her back, he grabbed her ass and scooped her up as he stood.

Hope gave a tiny sound of surprise as she was lifted, but she didn't pull away. Only when he lowered her onto the fold-down bed did she tear her mouth from his, looking up at him with wide brown eyes.

Kos searched her face, seeing both arousal and hesitation

behind her eyes. Her breathing was shallow, and her chest heaved beneath his.

"You are beautiful," he said, bracing his elbows on both sides of her and taking her face in his hands. He stroked his thumbs down her cheeks, marveling at the silky skin.

Her eyelids fluttered. "Kos."

Hearing his name from her lips made him growl low. Lowering his mouth to hers, he kissed her again—first gently and then more deeply—losing himself in the feel of her.

He'd heard talk on the Boat about the human females, and he'd seen plenty of them over the years. He'd always marveled at how different they were from each other—the color of their skin, the hue of their hair, the shape of their bodies—and he'd wondered what it would be like to touch one.

Now he knew, and it was better than he could have imagined. He didn't know why she'd changed her mind. Maybe she'd decided she didn't want to live on the reject side of the station, maybe it had sunk in that she wouldn't be returning to Earth, or maybe she'd just decided she liked the looks of him. For the moment, he didn't care why. He just cared that she was kissing him, her body moving beneath his.

Her legs parted as he settled himself on top of her, still holding the bulk of his weight on his elbows, but he felt her wrap her legs around the back of his and arch into him. His cock pulsed thick as he ground himself between her legs, hearing a high-pitched sigh escape her lips.

She tore her mouth from his, kissing his face and making her way to his ear, sucking hard on his earlobe and moaning. His eyes rolled back in his head, and his cock throbbed.

Gods, the female was driving him crazy with her noises—and her mouth. The thought of what else she could do with her mouth made him lightheaded.

Her fingers roamed across his back, and when she began stroking his nodes, Kos let out a deep rumble.

"You like that?" she asked, her voice a seductive purr. "I saw these while you were fighting. They're harder than I expected. And hotter."

"You make them hard," he told her. "And hot."

"Oh." She sounded intrigued as she tugged the back of his shirt up and slipped her hands underneath. "That's pretty wild. You don't have any other surprises for me, do you?"

He bowed his back as she rubbed her fingertips across his bare nodes, her touch scorching his flesh. "No more surprises."

"Well." She gyrated her hips so his cock rubbed between her legs. "I'd call this a pleasant surprise."

Kos's heart thumped so hard in his chest he thought it might actually explode. "Everything about you is a pleasant surprise."

She let out a throaty laugh. "If I didn't know better, I'd say you were trying to get in my pants, warrior."

He ran one hand down around her ass and up the back of her bent thigh, hitching it higher. "I do not think we would both fit in your pants. Maybe I should help you out of them."

She laughed again. "And then what?"

He locked his gaze on hers. "Then I bury my cock inside you and claim you as my mate."

Hope's dark pupils flared. "That's so caveman of you." She dug her fingernails into his back. "I like it."

"I want you to like it. I want you to like everything I do to you." He traced his thumb across her jawline. "I want to make you happy."

Her brow furrowed, and she bit the corner of her bottom lip. "I believe you, and I'm really sorry."

Kos tilted his head to one side. Why was she sorry? Did she regret what she'd said earlier? "You have nothing to be sorry for, *cinnara*."

She flinched at the Drexian term of endearment. "Yes, I do."

Kos didn't have time to wonder what she meant as she pulled him to her for another kiss. His head swirled with desire, his pulse hammering and his cock pulsating. By the time he noticed her hand moving to the blaster on his belt, she'd already unhooked it.

He jerked back as a sharp pain shot across the back of his head. He saw Hope's eyes go wide as he took another hit, then her face blurred, and everything went dark.

CHAPTER
TEN

Hope gasped as Kos collapsed on her, the full weight of his muscular body forcing the air out of her.

Great. Just fucking great. She was going to smother to death underneath him.

She jerked her body hard and managed to roll him toward the wall of the ship. After bashing him on the back of the skull with a blaster twice, the last thing she wanted to do was roll him onto the floor. She wanted to get back to Earth, but she didn't want to do serious damage to the guy.

Hope managed to wiggle herself out from under him, falling onto the hard floor herself, and her hands stinging from the impact. She stood, leaning over Kos and inspecting the knot on the back of his head.

She hadn't broken the skin—that was good—but there was a definite bump.

She felt a pang of regret that she'd hit the Drexian. "Like I said, I'm really sorry, mate. It's nothing personal."

Although, looking down at the warrior lying face-down on the bed, it felt pretty personal. After all, she'd purposely seduced him and then attacked him. Kos would not be happy when he came to.

She thought about his reaction when he realized what she'd done and cringed. It would not be good. Hope glanced around the shuttle. She needed to tie him up, otherwise her plan to get back to Earth would never work. The second he came to, he'd change course and probably take her straight to tribute bride jail, if they had such a thing.

She opened several of the panels lining the shuttle walls, revealing hidden cabinets. At first, all she found were ration packets and standard-issue Drexian clothing. Finally, she located the Drexian version of plastic zip ties.

Hope fastened his hands together and tied them, trying not to pull too hard. She still felt guilty for all of it and wished the guy didn't have to be so great. Or so hot.

She'd almost lost her nerve when he started saying all those sweet things to her, and she almost forgot her entire mission when he told her he wanted to bury his cock in her. Even thinking about it made her pulse quicken.

Focus, Hope, she told herself. *You're trying to get back home, not bone a really well-hung alien.*

With a final glance at Kos, she went to the ship's console. One major problem with her plan was that she didn't know how to fly an alien space shuttle and none of the symbols that flashed up at her made any sense.

"I don't suppose you have Siri capability?" she muttered to herself.

The ship didn't respond, not that she'd expected it to. She sat down in the pilot's chair and tried to remember what Kos had done when he'd set their course.

She tapped on the illuminated star chart, and it blinked a green arc across the shiny black screen. Okay, that's where they were going. But where was Earth? She squinted at the dots with symbols to the side "Which one of you little fuckers is Earth?"

On every map of the galaxy she'd ever seen, Earth was labeled clearly and often colored blue. More times than not, it was shown in the middle, making it even easier to find. She sighed as she scoured this chart. Of course, Earth wasn't the centerpiece of this map, nor was it conveniently color-coded.

"This is impossible," she said, banging her palms on the edge of the console and making it beep.

"What are you doing?" Kos's deep voice, sluggish and confused, made her jerk around.

He was coming to and twisting from side to side on the bed, tugging roughly at the zip ties binding his wrists at the small of his back.

Shit. He hadn't been out long, although she was also relieved she hadn't done any permanent damage. Considering how vigorously he was moving, he seemed to be just fine.

"Hope," he said, sharply. "Untie me."

"I'm really sorry, but I can't do that."

He growled, but it was not a sexy, spine-tingling growl. It was more of an animalistic, I'm-about-to-rip-your-throat-out kind of growl. "You do not know what you are doing."

Well, he was right about that. She definitely did not know how to get the shuttle to take her back to Earth. "All I want to do is go home. I have no intention of ever telling anyone about my little alien adventure. I just want to return to my old life and forget any of this ever happened."

"That is impossible," he said, rolling himself over and almost falling onto the floor.

"That's where you're wrong," she said, eyeing him and realizing she should have tied his feet as well. "All you have to do is help me chart a new course to Earth. Then you can drop me off, go home, and request a new tribute bride—one who actually wants to get married."

He jerked himself to sitting, his face flushed. "I do not want a new tribute bride."

Okay, it was official. The guy was nuts. Why would he still want her after she'd knocked him over the head with his own blaster?

"You know," she said, heat creeping up her neck as she turned to look at him, "this isn't only about what you want."

"And you do not want me?" His eyes flashed as they met hers. "I do not believe you."

Okay, maybe a part of her did want him. What woman wouldn't get turned on by a smoking hot man who was all muscles and had a huge cock? She was only human, after all. But that didn't mean she wanted to give up everything for him. "Believe me when I say I don't want to be anyone's tribute bride."

Kos stared at her, not blinking. "I cannot take you back to Earth."

"Yeah, I know. That's why I'm piloting the ship now."

He raised one eyebrow. "You do not know how to pilot a Drexian ship." He glanced at the console. "Our course has not changed."

"It's only a matter of time before I figure it out." She knew that was not actually true. It was entirely possible that they could fly along for days before she figured out how to plot a course to Earth.

Both his eyebrows popped up and he leaned back against the wall of the shuttle. "Fine. I will wait while you take us to Earth."

Hope shot him a dirty look. The cocky bastard knew very well she couldn't do it, and he was going to wait her out. Since they were currently flying on autopilot, there was a very real possibility that they'd arrive at the Drexian outpost with her sitting in the pilot's chair still trying to figure it out and him tied up on the bed. She knew that would not go so well for her.

She swung her gaze back to the console. She'd show him. Tapping her fingers on a series of buttons, she yelped as the ship slammed to a stop. Hope braced herself on the console so she wouldn't fly forward, and she heard a thump behind her.

Glancing back, she saw that Kos had landed on the floor. She cringed as she watched him moan and roll over. "Sorry about that."

"What have you done?" he said between gritted teeth.

She peered out the front of the ship. Instead of the slashes of light zipping past them, they appeared to be hovering motionless in space. To one side was an orange planet or moon, its surface bright and shifting. "I think I hit the brakes."

Kos sat up, shaking his head. "We need to start moving again. We do not want to stop in this sector, especially with our stealth shielding deactivated."

Hope swiveled her head to him. "Why not?"

"Trust me," was the only answer he gave her.

Her stomach fluttered. "Okay, so how do I get us going again and activate the stealth whatever?"

"Untie me."

She gnawed at her lower lip. "No way. You'll take me right back to the Drexian station or outpost or wherever."

"Hope, listen to me. I have to get you to safety." His voice sounded almost pleading, and her resolve wavered.

Before she could agree to untie him, another jolt made her slip off the chair. She hit the floor next to Kos. "What the hell was that?"

The shuttle lurched forward as Hope scrambled to her feet. "We're moving. I don't know how, but we're moving backward."

Kos's lips became a white line. "It's a tractor beam."

"A what?" Her gut tightened.

"We're being pulled by another ship. A bigger ship."

Hope thought about what he'd said about not stopping in that sector. She didn't think she wanted to know what kind of bigger ship was pulling them. Their speed increased, and they were drawn into a large metal hangar bay. They landed with a jolt that rattled her teeth.

"You need to untie me," he said again, and this time his voice was low and urgent as the ramp to their shuttle lowered.

Nodding, she went to him. Her heart was pounding and her hands shaking as she tugged at the zip tie before realizing she needed to cut it off. She pulled the blade off his belt, giving him an apologetic look. "Hold still."

"It is you who needs to hold still," a sharp voice said.

Hope looked up and saw a large weapon trained on her, the red-skinned alien behind it smiling as she tossed her long black hair off her shoulders.

CHAPTER

ELEVEN

K os bristled as two beefy aliens in body armor pulled him to his feet. Hope had managed to slice partially through his restraints before she'd been forced to drop the blade, and he could feel the give of the ties as his wrists strained against them.

Hope.

He craned his neck to find the human female, letting out a breath of relief when he saw that she was walking freely behind him. Although the red-skinned alien held the weapon at her back, her hands had not been bound. Her eyes were downcast as she walked, and he suspected she felt responsible for the mess they were in.

Which she was, he reminded himself. If she hadn't knocked him out, tied him up, and pulled the shuttle out of warp, they'd still be on their way to the Drexian outpost. He felt like shaking her—hard. He also felt like wrapping his arms around her and telling her that everything was going to be alright.

They walked through the hangar deck and onto the main part of the ship. Kos still couldn't tell what kind of ship they'd been taken by since he hadn't seen the vessel, but as they walked out of the hangar deck, his stomach clenched.

The ship appeared to be a giant cylinder that spiraled up from the bottom. White and gleaming, it reminded him somewhat of the Boat—sleek and modern and almost uncomfortably bright. A single ramp swirled up and circled the perimeter of the ship with clear bridges crossing the center and connecting the sides.

As they were led up the ramp, the ball in Kos's gut hardened. The ship was like a cross between a museum and a prison. Clear compartments lined the ramp, and each appeared to contain a different type of alien. Some sat on the beds, some paced, some stared out at their window overlooking space. But all of them looked like captives.

Kos recognized a few species—Crelpies with spikes along their spines, Hathrings covered in so much fluffy blue fur it was impossible to make out their faces, Tartules with tentacles for hands—and flinched when he spotted the familiar form of a Gatazoid in one of the cells. What kind of twisted zoo was this?

When they reached the center of the ship, the armed aliens prodded him toward a platform extending into the middle. Stepping through a door, Kos saw that the room suspended in the center of the ship had curved white walls. Floor-to-ceiling shelving units arched around the walls with artifacts displayed prominently. Kos didn't have time to study the objects before his eyes settled on a purple-skinned alien sitting on a throne-like chair in the center.

He had spiky white hair and colorless eyes, which blinked rapidly when they landed on Kos. "Come in, come in. You are most welcome."

The red-skinned female with the mane of black hair prodded Hope until she stood next to him. "For your approval, Curator."

Kos's mouth went dry. The Curator? He'd heard of the notorious alien but had always assumed most of the tales about him were fabricated. A Tyrithian—one of the last of his kind—who roamed the universe collecting various aliens had seemed too grotesque to be true. Even more unbelievable were the stories about the parties he hosted to display his collection. It was said that he charged enormous sums for the wealthiest aliens to come aboard and view his collection. Interacting with the aliens on display was extra but encouraged.

Kos felt bile rise in his throat as the Curator rose from his chair and approached them, rubbing his hands together.

"Delightful," he said, his smile almost impish. "What are they?"

The red-skinned female glanced down at her scanner. "A Drexian and a...human."

The Curator giggled. "I've always wanted a Drexian for the collection." He reached out a hand and let it hover only millimeters over Kos's bicep. "This is quite a find."

Kos resisted the urge to recoil. He could not let the creature know how disgusted he was, or how rattled.

The Curator pivoted toward Hope and tilted his head. "I've never heard of a hu-man before. Where are they from, Zaria?"

The female apparently called Zaria shrugged. "A non-warp planet called Earth. It's protected by the Drexians. It's where they get their mates."

The Curator's face lit up, and he snapped his fingers. "That's right. I heard about that. The females they take from an unsophisticated planet." He leaned closer to Hope. "Unusual looking, aren't they?"

Hope leaned back, bumping into Kos. "Look who's talking, you wanker."

The Curator giggled again. "Earthians are feisty."

"Earthlings," Hope corrected, mumbling 'wanker' under her breath again.

The Curator cocked a white eyebrow and bowed slightly. "My apologies, Earth*ling*." He spun on his heel and walked back to his oversized chair, flicking his gaze to Zaria. "So, are these two mated?"

Zaria nudged Hope hard in the ribs. "Answer the Curator. Are you his mate?"

"Not officially, no. I mean, I'm not anyone's mate," Hope stammered, cutting a quick glance to Kos.

The Curator leaned forward and narrowed his eyes, shifting his gaze between Hope and Kos. He finally flopped back. "I don't believe you. Why else would a human and a Drexian be on a shuttle together?"

"He was taking me back to Earth," Hope said, ignoring Kos's sharp look. "I barely know him."

"He was tied up when we found them," Zaria said, stifling a laugh.

The Curator's eyes brightened. "Tied up? Indeed? Oh, I like that." He steepled his fingers and drummed them against each other. "That would go over very well with my guests, although I suspect they would prefer to see the female tied up."

Kos suppressed an urge to lunge at the alien. He wanted to rip the giddy man's arms off for talking about Hope like she was some sort of object to be played with.

The Curator glanced back at Kos and smiled. "Yes, he's clearly her mate. I've heard about big, tough Drexians and how possessive they are about their little humans."

"She is not mine," Kos forced himself to say. He knew what would happen if this collector decided they were a couple. "It is as she said. I was merely her pilot."

The Curator smiled at him, the boyish grin making him appear almost harmless. "You're lying." He waved a hand in front of himself. "I don't blame you. You're trying to protect her."

Zaria chuckled behind them.

"Of course, if you're not together," the Curator continued, "we could always put her in a case with a Xalurian." His clear eyes seemed to glow silver. "They're insatiable."

Hope made a small noise, moving closer to him.

"That's what I thought," the Curator said. He nodded to Zaria.

"Put them in one of our premium cases. They'll be the main attraction at our next party."

The two armored aliens took him by the arms and led him out of the room. His face burned, but he tried to keep his breathing steady. They needed to get out of there, preferably before they were shoved into a cell. He scanned the ship as they were led further up the spiraling ramp. Aside from the guards with them, he didn't see any more armed aliens he needed to contend with.

He tested the zip ties again. One sharp snap should do it. Then he'd have to take out the two guards and the red-skinned alien before they would have to run down the entire length of the ramp to get to the hangar deck and their shuttle.

As they reached a clear-fronted compartment, Kos steeled himself. It was now or never. With a hard yank, he snapped off the zip ties binding his wrists and spun around. Both his blaster and blade were gone, but he quickly knocked the oversized blaster out of Zaria's hand, and it skittered across the floor.

Zaria screamed, but Kos had already knocked one of the burly alien guards off his feet by kicking his kneecaps in, and he fired a quick blow to the other's throat. Grabbing a gaping Hope by the hand, he ran down the ramp, scooping up Zaria's blaster before she could reach it.

He fired the weapon over his shoulder, running as fast as he could. To her credit, Hope matched him step for step. They'd almost reached the bottom, when his entire body convulsed. It felt like electricity was shooting up from the floor. Kos dropped the weapon as his body jerked. He could feel Hope twitching next to him, and he didn't know if it was her screams that tore through the air or his.

When the pain stopped, they both sank to the floor, their bodies spasming. Kos tried to push himself up, but his muscles would not cooperate. He saw a pair of black, pointed-toe boots approaching and stop next to his face.

"That was a mistake," Zaria said before lifting one foot and kicking him hard.

CHAPTER

TWELVE

H ope blinked up at the shiny white ceiling. Why was it so bright? And why did she feel like throwing up?

Rolling over, she saw a pair of large, emerald green eyes watching her. Her breath caught in her throat until she realized that the creature with the large eyes was on the other side of a plexiglass wall.

"You okay?" the creature asked, her voice a near purr.

Hope pushed herself up until she was sitting cross-legged and facing the alien in the adjoining cell. "I think so."

The creature had yellow skin covered in a fine downy fur and a long tail she held in one hand. "They got you pretty good with the electrified floor panels."

Hope rubbed her bare arms. "So that's what that was." Even the memory of the jolts that had made her body convulse sent a fresh wave of nausea through her.

"You'll feel the aftereffects for a while," the alien told her, "but you shouldn't sustain any permanent damage."

"Good to know," Hope muttered.

Peering around, she saw that she was in one of the compartments that ringed the spaceship. Three sides were clear, and the only solid white wall had a rectangular window that looked out into space. Instead of a single bed pushed up against one side, this room had a larger bed in the middle. Craning her neck even more, she saw that Kos was lying behind her, his knees pulled into his chest in a near-fetal position.

"Zaria made sure he was out of commission before they moved him again," the neighbor said.

Hope touched a hand tentatively to his arm, but he didn't respond. "How did she do that?"

The alien worked the fluffy end of her tail and shook her head. "You don't want to know."

Hope rested her hand on the Drexian's arm. This was all her fault. If she hadn't been so hell-bent on getting home, they'd both be safe. She may not be where she wanted to be, but Kos wouldn't be injured, and they wouldn't be in a weird prison being held by a super creepy alien who had a voyeurism fetish. She shuddered as she thought about what he'd said.

She and Kos were supposed to be the main attraction at some party. She didn't know exactly what that meant, but she knew it couldn't be good. She glanced down at the unconscious Drexian.

"I'm so sorry," she whispered. "I know you'll probably never forgive me for all this, but I really am sorry." She flashed back to the look of betrayal in his eyes when he'd found himself tied up and realized she'd manipulated him. She may have regretted that most of all. "For everything."

"I doubt he can hear you," the alien next door said. "But I'm sure he'll forgive you. He's your mate, right?"

"It's complicated," Hope said.

The woman gave a nervous laugh. "I'm afraid it's only going to get more complicated in here."

Hope pulled her gaze from Kos and focused on the female alien. "Have you been in here long?"

"Long enough." She pulled on the end of her tail. "I'm Xarla."

Hope tried to mimic the hard "ch" sound at the front of the alien's name. "Hi Xarla. I'm Hope."

Xarla glanced at Kos. "And the Drexian?"

"Kos," Hope said.

"How did they get you?" Xarla asked.

Hope took a shuddering breath. "It's my fault we're here. I wanted to go back to my home, Earth, so I knocked out Kos and commandeered the shuttle."

Xarla's vivid green eyes widened.

"The trouble was, I didn't know how to fly it and I'd tied up Kos. I ended up taking the ship out of warp and bringing us to a standstill. I guess that's when this ship saw us and decided to pull us in with a tractor beam."

"Oh." Xarla twisted her tail. "Now I understand why you were apologizing to him."

"Yeah." Hope heard her voice crack. "I'm pretty sure he hates me."

"For your sake, I hope he doesn't. The Curator's guests don't want to watch a couple fighting."

Hope swallowed hard. "What do they want to watch?"

Xarla looked down. "It depends. I'm a Vralithian." She paused as if this should mean something.

Hope assessed the cat-like creature. "Sorry, I'm not familiar with alien species and what they're known for. What does that mean?"

"I'm very flexible," Xarla said. "I can twist myself into all sorts of configurations."

"Wow. It doesn't hurt?"

Xarla stood, arching her back and coming up between her own legs, then placing her hands on the floor and whipping her legs back around. "No. I have a floating spine."

Hope didn't know what that meant, but she suspected alien anatomy was a lot different from humans. "So, everyone has to perform during the parties?"

Xarla settled herself on the floor and wrapped her tail around her shoulders and shrugged. "That part isn't so bad. It's getting picked by one of the guests that you don't want."

Hope's pulse quickened. "I'm guessing that means you have a private party with them?"

Xarla's eyes went to the floor. "It's better than getting the end of Zaria's whip."

"Whip?"

"Zaria patrols the parties for the Curator. Makes sure all the guests are getting what they paid for. If anyone isn't happy, she uses her laser whip."

"That's barbaric," Hope said.

Another shrug from Xarla. "Who's going to stop her?"

"Aren't there some sort of space laws to prevent this kind of thing? This can't be legal. "

"Not in this sector there aren't. That's why aliens come here from all over. They can get away with things they never could in other places."

"If the Drexians find out about this, they're going to make the Curator sorry he was ever born."

"I'm afraid the chances of your Drexians finding you are slim," Xarla said. "The Curator has the sector's enforcers in his pocket. The ones he isn't blackmailing, that is. He pays handsomely to keep his location secret."

"And no one ever escapes?" Hope asked.

"The only way anyone gets off is if they're bought. But that doesn't happen often."

Hope let out a breath. This was why she was a loner, she thought. Whenever she got involved with someone, they ended up getting hurt. She looked over at Kos as he stirred, dreading explaining everything to him and dreading how furious he was going to be.

CHAPTER

THIRTEEN

"Kos?" The female's face came into view, although it took him a few moments to remember exactly where they were and why he was lying on the floor. And why he felt so drained and shaky.

He sat up, his head swimming. "Are you okay?"

She nodded. "I'm fine." She reached a hand tentatively and touched his arm. "What about you?"

He glanced around at the pristine cell with its bright lights and transparent walls, clenching his jaw when he spotted the large bed. He was far from fine.

He stood, ignoring the tingling in his limbs, and walked the perimeter of the room. He scanned the ceiling for vents and saw nothing large enough to fit through. At least, nothing he could squeeze through. There was a gap at the top of the clear walls between the cells, but only for ventilation, and it was too narrow for anyone but a child to fit through, if that. Even extending his arms, he could barely touch it.

Pressing his palms to the sliding panel that was the door and front of the cell, he leaned hard. Nothing. No give and no buckling. Whatever the transparent substance was, it wasn't going to be easy

65

to break. He rapped his knuckles on it as he thought about how he was going to get them out.

Kos *was* going to get them out. He had to. The alternative—spending the rest of their lives as part of some living collection—was not an option.

"Kos?" Hope's voice jerked him out of his thoughts.

He spun around. "What?" The word came out harsher than he'd intended, and the female flinched.

"What are you doing?" she asked.

"What does it look like? I'm trying to figure out a way to escape."

A sound came from the next cell, and he looked over to see a creature sitting on the floor with her tail draped around her shoulders. She'd been so motionless he hadn't noticed her until she made a sound.

"This is Xarla," Hope said, sweeping a hand in the alien's direction. "She's been telling me about this place."

Kos gave her a curt nod before turning his attention back to the door.

"No one's ever escaped," Xarla said.

Kos looked back at her, noticing how she nervously stroked her tail. He noticed that the cell on the other side of them was unoccupied, so for the moment, she was his only source of information. "Not yet."

Xarla let out a small laugh that died quickly. "The Curator designed this place to be impossible to break out of. Bigger creatures than you have tried."

Kos thought of some of the fearsome aliens he'd seen as they'd walked around the spiraling ramp. He might have spent hours upon hours training for battle, but he didn't have spikes shooting out of his spine or horns jutting from his forehead.

"*Grek,*" he cursed.

"Listen, Kos." Hope joined him at the door. "I'm really sorry about all this."

He grunted but didn't respond. He knew the nice thing to do would be to accept her apology and tell her that everything would be okay. He just didn't feel like lying.

"I know this is all my fault..." she continued.

He whirled on her. "Yes, it is."

Her eyes widened, and she stepped back.

"Being rescued from the Ganthar wasn't enough for you, was it?" His voice rose. "You couldn't just say thank you."

Color flooded her cheeks, but she pursed her lips and scrunched them to one side. "Oh, I'm sorry. Did I not thank you enough for taking me off my home planet against my will? Unfortunately, there isn't a 'thanks for abducting me and forcing me to marry a total stranger' Hallmark card for that, or I definitely would have given it to you."

Kos didn't know what most of that meant, but he understood enough. "I get it. You hate the idea of being matched with me."

She let out an impatient huff. "It's not you. Like I said, it wasn't personal."

He stepped closer to her and their bodies almost touched. "Really? It felt pretty personal when you had your legs wrapped around my waist."

Xarla sucked in a breath, but Kos didn't let his gaze leave Hope, whose eyes were flashing dangerously, her head tipped back to look at him. Even though he towered over her, she hadn't backed away.

"That's why you're really upset, isn't it?" she asked. "Because I tricked you."

His heart raced. Even though he could feel his ire rising, heat also coiled at the base of his spine as he watched her chest rise and fall. "I'm upset because we're trapped in this prison with no way out. No one knows we're here. Since I was tied up at the time, I wasn't able to get off a distress call."

She cringed at that. "I'm sorry I tied you up. I had no idea our ship would be intercepted and we'd be taken prisoner."

"Of course, you didn't. Because you have no idea about this

sector or about space or flying a shuttlecraft." His voice grew louder. "All things you should have thought about before you disabled me and caused our ship to be dead in the water."

"Fine." She threw her hands up. "I get it. I'm impulsive and thoughtless and selfish. Don't think I haven't heard it all before. This is exactly why I'm not good mate material. I'm not a team player. I do better on my own. That way the only person who gets hurt when I do something really dumb is me."

He wanted to shake her, but he saw the hurt in her eyes and suspected she'd been the one hurt more often than she wanted to let on. Kos released a breath and took a step back.

"Well, none of that matters now because we're officially stuck with each other in here." He spread his arms wide. "I'm afraid there's no escaping me."

She was silent for a moment, and he wondered if that fact was just now sinking in. If she'd been trying to get away from him, she'd achieved the opposite.

"Won't the other Drexians come looking for us when we don't show up?" she asked. "You came after me."

He shot her a side-eye glance and muttered, "Look where that got me."

She ignored his comment. "My point is that the Drexians seem pretty good at the whole search and rescue thing. They won't let one of their warriors or one of their oh-so-important tribute brides be lost forever."

Kos thought she might be right, but he also knew it would take a while before they were determined to be missing and even longer for warriors to search the space between here and the Drexian outpost. He suspected that the Curator was skilled at staying hidden. It was why he'd only heard whispers about the alien, and why he'd never been stopped before. Clearly, the Curator wasn't reckless.

"No time soon," he said, nodding to Xarla. "Your friend is right. We probably won't be able to break out by force."

"So, we just wait to be rescued?" Hope asked. "I guess I can do that."

He cocked his head at her. "Now you're willing to be patient?"

She glared at him. "I said I was sorry. I'm sorry for getting us into this mess, and I'm sorry if I hurt your feelings."

Kos narrowed his gaze at her. "You think I am concerned about my feelings?"

She shrugged. "I don't know. Maybe you're just irritated that you didn't get some. You probably thought I was a sure thing, huh?"

"A sure thing?"

She stalked over to him. "It means you thought we were going to fuck, and you're mad we didn't."

Anger flared in his chest, and he clenched his fists. Was that really what she thought about him? That he only wanted her for sex? Did she really not understand that he wanted her for much more? That he wanted to bind himself to her for life?

He steadied his breath and locked eyes with her. "I am not mad at you for that, although I will not deny that I desire you. But if you wanted to make sure I did not claim you, then you made a serious mistake getting us thrown in here."

Hope swallowed hard, her gaze darting to the single large bed that was the centerpiece of the room.

He leaned down so that his lips brushed the tip of her earlobe. "Why do you think the Curator put us in here together? Didn't you hear him say we're to be the featured attraction at his next party?"

"Yes," she stammered, "but..." Her words drifted off and her cheeks flushed pink.

"Well, pretty human," he said, feeling her trembling. "That means we're going to have quite an audience the first time I claim you as my mate."

CHAPTER
FOURTEEN

Hope stared up at the ceiling with her arms crossed. Kos's big body next to her made the bed sag toward him, but she resisted the pull, staying firmly on her side. If his steady, heavy breathing was any indication, the Drexian was fast asleep.

How could he sleep? She felt like kicking him to wake him, but she knew her irritation was irrational. Why shouldn't he get some sleep? It wasn't like any of this was his fault, after all. He could probably sleep like a baby while she lay there replaying in her mind all the stupid things she'd done that had landed her in her current predicament.

She blew out a breath. It wasn't like it was the first time she'd screwed things up. Only this time, she'd sucked someone else into her mess. Someone who didn't deserve it.

She turned her head to look at the massive body next to her. Even though the lights had been dimmed, ambient light still spilled in from the hallway, making it easy to make out his profile. She looked away quickly. Even asleep, the guy was hot.

At least when he was asleep she didn't have to see the look of betrayal in his eyes every time he glanced at her. Maybe she was imagining it, but she wouldn't blame him if he hated her forever. She might hate someone if they'd ruined her life, especially if she'd fought to free them.

She squeezed her eyes closed. Kos was right. Why couldn't she have been grateful? Why had she been so determined to get away?

Because running is what you do, a little voice whispered to her.

"Shut up," she whispered back. She didn't *always* run, although she did like to keep moving. But that was more a result of being a travel blogger than anything else.

A job you like because it keeps you from putting down roots.

"Seriously?" she mumbled to herself. "Where was this insight when I was deciding to commandeer a space shuttle?"

Even if it was true that she had a problem staying in one place, she came by it honestly. Her mother had taken off when she was a kid, preferring to bum around with a shaman instead of doing the messy work of being a mom. Hope had gotten over it, but she'd learned never to rely on anyone to stick around. It was easier to keep moving, which made her current situation even more uncomfortable.

Now, she was literally trapped in a cell with a guy. She couldn't leave if she wanted to, and neither could he. They were officially stuck with each other. If she'd been put out by the idea of an arranged marriage, imprisonment and forced copulation was taking it to a whole new level.

Hope twisted restlessly, trying to push thoughts of what they might be forced to do out of her head. There had to be a way around it, because the alternative...? She shivered and rubbed her arms.

Kos drew in a deep breath and rolled over to face her. She closed her eyes and willed herself to fall asleep, telling herself that she was back on Earth. But the sounds of the other prisoners sleeping made it impossible for her to forget where she was. How did people ever sleep in prison, she wondered? The sound of labored snoring came from somewhere farther down the hall, but the rhythmic purring from Xarla was much harder to ignore.

TANA STONE

Huffing out a breath, she opened her eyes again. That's when she felt him staring at her and turned her head to see that Kos was awake.

"You should try to sleep," he said.

She put a hand to her fast-beating heart. "You startled me. I thought you were asleep."

"I was. You move a lot."

"Sorry. It's hard to sleep with all the noise."

Kos angled his head, as if listening. "Now I hear it. I suppose I got used to sleeping through things when I was at the Drexian military academy."

"I've slept in enough hostels that you'd think I'd be used to snoring," Hope said, "but I've never slept in a prison before."

"Are you afraid?" he asked.

Before she could think better of it, she said, "Of course I'm afraid. Aren't you?"

"I do not think the Curator will hurt us or starve us," he said, touching a hand gently to the side of her face. "I am only scared for you."

His soft touch felt scalding, and her pulse fluttered wildly. "For me?"

"I do not want anyone seeing you." A muscle ticked along his jawline. "The idea of males watching you is unacceptable, even if they are watching you with me."

She tried to swallow but her throat felt thick. "Maybe we can trick them. Convince them we're doing things we're not."

He raised an eyebrow. "I do not know how we would do that."

She sighed. "Yeah, me neither. And Xarla said that the crazy red-skinned bitch Zaria uses a laser whip if you don't perform like they want you to."

Kos growled low, and Hope felt the rumble in her chest.

"It will be okay," he said, cupping her face in his hand. "I will not let anyone touch you."

She loved that he was still willing to defend her, even after she'd totally screwed him over and landed them both in a weird alien zoo jail. Of course, she knew that he would only be able to do so much. The Curator and his goons were the ones with the whips and the electrified floors and who knew what else. Even a badass Drexian warrior was outmatched when it came to those things.

She turned so that she faced him fully and wiggled closer to him, enjoying the heat that radiated off his body. Kos moved his hand from her face down to her hip, tugging her even closer until their bodies were flush.

"I'm really sorry, you know," she whispered.

"I know." He moved his hand back to her face, brushing a loose strand off her forehead. "This is not your world. You did not understand the consequences."

"Maybe, but I shouldn't have tricked you and knocked you out. That wasn't cool."

A smile teased the edge of his mouth. "No, it was not, as you say, cool. But I could have tried not to scare you into accepting me."

She peered up at him. "I keep telling you, my freaking out really had nothing to do with you. It's totally my deal. If I wasn't such a commitment-phobe, I'd be all over you and the whole tribute bride deal."

His eyebrow quirked.

Hope placed a hand on his chest. "I'm not just saying that because we're locked in a room together."

A small laugh escaped his throat. "No?"

She grinned and shook her head. "Nope. Trust me. If I couldn't stand you, I wouldn't care if we were strapped together back-to-back. I still wouldn't be nice to you."

"Thank you, I think."

"To be honest," she said, "you're exactly my type. I mean, look at you. You're any woman's type. Tall, dark, and built." She gave her head a small shake. She'd had a point, right? "But you're also not a dick, which is a big plus."

"Again, thank you."

She slapped his chest lightly. "You know what I mean. I've been involved with a lot of guys who weren't very nice, probably because they were exactly the type not to want to stick around either. That's one problem with picking men who won't get attached. They're usually not great guys."

"I do not understand why you would want to select a mate who would leave."

She wrinkled her nose. "I wasn't picking a mate. I was just having fun, dating, you know."

He shook his head. "Drexians do not date. We occasionally visit the pleasure planets, but that is purely recreational."

"Well, then the men I used to date were purely recreational, too," Hope said. "I never even thought about settling down or getting married."

"Is that not unusual on Earth?" Kos asked. "To never get married."

She squirmed a bit. "It's not *that* unusual. I guess most people don't decide not to get married. They just don't ever find the right person."

"But you decided?"

"That's right. I didn't know anyone who'd been happily married. My parents weren't, that's for sure. And when my friends got divorced, it totally sucked for them. It's easier to avoid all that heartbreak by never falling in love or getting married in the first place."

"And now?" He rested his hand over her smaller one pressed to his chest. "If we get rescued, you would still choose to reject our match and be alone?"

Hope's mouth was dry. Would she? After everything, would she really tell the guy to take a hike? She wanted to tell him that she'd changed, but she knew she hadn't. The thought of one guy forever still made panic flutter in her chest. "I...I don't know."

The flicker of hope in his eyes dimmed, and he pulled his hand away from hers.

CHAPTER

FIFTEEN

W hat did he expect? Kos thought, sitting up. The female had been perfectly clear. Did he really think she would change her mind so easily? She struck him as more than a little stubborn.

The back of his neck prickled, and he squinted across at the clear wall. The Curator stood on the other side, his hands behind his back as he rocked on his heels.

"Don't let me interrupt you," the Curator said, his voice low and seductive. It made Kos stifle the urge to shudder.

Kos stood quickly, glancing back at the bed. "Like I told you before, we are not together. I was only the pilot taking her back to my people."

The Curator shook his head slowly as he tapped a finger on his chin. "I do not think so. I know all about you Drexians, although you are the first specimen I've been able to obtain."

Kos flinched. Of course, he was the first of his kind to be taken. Drexian warriors were not known for being taken by surprise. They were also rarely knocked out and tied up by those they were trying to save. He almost dreaded his people discovering this shameful capture as much as he dreaded being held captive.

The Curator smiled at him, the expression spreading across his face and giving him that wide-eyed look that seemed so out of place for a twisted criminal. "No, Drexians are very territorial about their females. If this one wasn't yours, you would not look at her the way you do."

Kos swallowed hard. "I assure you; she is not mine. This human has chosen not to take a Drexian mate. I was taking her back so she could join the other females who have rejected their matches."

The Curator's already wide eyes popped open even more. "You don't say? You really have no claim on this female?"

"None," Kos said.

"So, you would have no problem with me moving her into a display case with another exhibit? Perhaps the Krelpies, although I'd hate for her to get hurt so soon." The Curator's eyes danced. "You do know they have a spike at the end of their phallus? No problem for Krelpie females, but it might not be that pleasant for the human."

Kos squeezed his hands into fists. "Leave her alone."

The Curator let out a high-pitched laugh. "Oh, I have no intention of touching a hair on her pretty head. But my guests do require entertainment. If I don't provide enough diversions for them, they'll be most unhappy. And if they're unhappy ..."

"When my people find me, you will regret not letting us go," Kos growled.

The Curator shrugged. "Many have tried to find me."

Kos wondered just how the alien had avoided being tracked down for so long. Surely a floating zoo prison wasn't tough to track, and he knew the ship wasn't cloaked. The Drexians were the only ones to have effective cloaking technology. The Curator must pay a great deal in protection money to keep his whereabouts hidden.

It didn't matter, though. The Drexians would find him, especially if they used the Inferno Force trackers. He knew Inferno Force had never turned their attentions to tracking down the Curator. They'd never had a reason, and they'd never known exactly what was going on. But if they discovered that a Drexian warrior and a tribute bride had been taken? Nothing would stop them from finding the Curator's ship. Of course, it was small comfort now, when he knew it might be days before they were reported missing.

"The Drexians have never tried to hunt you down," Kos said. "Until now."

The Curator flinched slightly but his smile remained. "In that case, it is good that I have a party planned for tomorrow evening. If you and the human won't be with us for long, it will make the event even more exclusive." He rubbed his hands together. "Yes, I think I'll have to increase the cost, as well. This will be a once in a lifetime experience." He leaned closer to the glass. "A Drexian warrior and a human female. Together. For only one night."

Kos's stomach tightened. He wanted to lunge for the alien, but it wouldn't do any good, and he did not want the creature to know that he'd gotten under his skin. He steadied his voice, trying to make it sound as light and conversational as the Curator's. "And if we decline to attend your party?"

Another laugh from the Curator. "The parties are not optional for the residents in my collection. I'm afraid I require full participation. Can you imagine if I let everyone make their own choices? Why, no one would ever agree to anything slightly distasteful or uncomfortable."

"I don't suppose you ever do anything that makes you uncomfortable?" Kos asked, taking long steps toward the clear wall dividing them.

"Why would I? I'm the Curator." The alien took a step back as Kos reached the glass and towered over him. "You should understand power and control, Drexian. What you do is not so different."

Kos bristled. "What we do?"

The Curator's gaze flicked to the bed. "I know all about your treaty and about the females you take. How is that any different than this?"

Kos knew the alien was goading him, but he could not resist

snapping back. "We do not force mating on anyone. And we would never make any female perform. That is dishonorable."

"To you, maybe," the Curator said. "The entire galaxy does not share the same code, you know. What is dishonorable to you is a natural pleasure to me."

Kos wished he could break through the wall and squeeze the life out of the arrogant alien. Instead, he took in a deep breath. "You will not have your pleasures for much longer, I promise you."

The Curator giggled. "You look so menacing when you make threats. I might have you do that as part of your performance this evening. I have some guests who enjoy pain with their pleasure, and threats from a Drexian warrior would be quite arousing."

Kos tried to make his face expressionless even as his voice was a dark whisper. "My threats are not idle."

The Curator gave an exaggerated shiver. "Perfect. Just perfect." His smile slipped as he locked eyes with Kos. "So, should I leave the human with you and trust you to perform, or should I partner her with a creature I know will give an enthusiastic performance?"

Kos despised the choice, but he knew he would rather have Hope with him than with some unknown alien. "Leave her with me."

"Are you sure?" The Curator shifted from one foot to the other. "I have a Langarian who hasn't been with a female in ages."

"I'm sure," Kos said. "As you said, who doesn't want to witness a Drexian and a human? Our pairings are legendary."

"So true," the Curator agreed, bouncing up and down on his heels. "This party will be all anyone will be talking about."

The light began to grow brighter, and the Curator clapped his hands. "Time to start our preparations."

As the alien bustled off up the winding hallway, Kos rested his palms on the clear wall, cursing to himself. He had a matter of hours to figure out how he and Hope were going to escape.

CHAPTER

SIXTEEN

H ope had stayed silent during the exchange between Kos and the Curator, glad that the room was so dimly lit. She hoped the Curator couldn't see that she was awake and listening. She didn't want him to notice her anger or her fear.

At first she'd felt hurt that Kos was going to such lengths to distance himself from her. Yes, she'd made it clear she wasn't down with being matched with him, but he seemed to be making a big point of not being with her. To save her, she reminded herself. He was trying to convince the Curator so they wouldn't be forced to perform together, although she would rather be with him than some unknown alien.

The thought of some creature with a spiked dick almost made her entire body start to shake, but she made sure not to move. She had a feeling that the Curator would love it if she showed any kind of fear. He seemed like a sadistic fuck, despite his sugary smiles and his weird child-like expressions.

Kos's conversation with the white-haired Curator didn't do anything to calm her fears. She wouldn't be forced to do anything with any of the other aliens, but that meant she and Kos were officially a couple. A performing couple, at least.

She swallowed hard, her pulse fluttering in her chest. It wasn't like she didn't find the big Drexian attractive. She did. And she'd never considered herself a prude, either. But it was a pretty big leap from thinking a guy was hot and not minding the idea of hooking up with him to putting on some sort of sex show.

She studied Kos's tall form as he stood at the glass, watching the Curator walk away, his arms folded tightly over his chest.

"So, humans and Drexians are legendary?" she asked, trying to make her voice light.

Kos twisted to look at her. "Do not worry. I will find a way to get us out before... I will find a way out of here."

Hope scooted to the edge of the bed. "I know you're supposed to be a super warrior, but have you taken a look around you? This is like some sort of crazy space super max prison. Xarla said no one has ever broken out."

"Just because no one has done it, doesn't mean it can't be done."

Before she could argue that sometimes it meant *exactly* that, Zaria appeared with a smile almost as wide as those of the Curator. The red-skinned alien extended a finger, pointed it at Hope, then curled it and beckoned her forward.

"You're with me, pretty," she said.

Hope didn't move from the edge of the bed, and she noticed Kos move his body so that he was between the two women.

Zaria frowned and shook her head, her black hair swinging slightly. "Don't make me come and get you. I promise you it won't be pleasant."

"What do you want with her?" Kos asked, not moving.

"Relax, Drexian. I'm taking her to be prepped for the party." Zaria rolled her eyes. "I promise I'll bring her back just like she was. Better, in fact. We're going to bathe her and dress her and get her all ready for you, big guy." Her gaze shifted to Kos and raked hungrily over his body. "Any preferences we should know about? Would you like us to pierce anything while we're at it?"

Hope let out an unwilling sound of protest, but Zaria threw back her head and laughed.

"I do not want her maimed or harmed in any way," Kos said, his voice a dark rumble.

Zaria huffed out a breath. "No fun at all. I thought you Drexians would be a lot wilder than you are." She cocked an eyebrow. "Although, I haven't seen you in action. Maybe I'll change my opinion after tonight."

Kos growled, one side of his lip curling.

Even though Hope's stomach was in knots, she stood. "It's okay," she told him. "I'm sure I'll be fine. They don't want to damage the new star of their show, right?"

Kos caught her hand as she walked past him. "Hope..."

She met his gaze, and her mouth went dry. The lights weren't at full brightness yet, but she could see the intensity in his eyes. His hand was warm and solid holding hers. She didn't want to let it go, but she knew she had to. She gave him a smile and squeezed his hand gently. "I'll be back before you can miss me."

She cut her eyes to Zaria, who was now tapping one foot impatiently, then looked back at Kos. His body almost vibrated with frustration, and she could see his shoulder muscles bunch.

She didn't know why she did it, but Hope leaned forward, raising herself up onto her tiptoes, and kissed him lightly on the lips. It didn't last more than a second, but her lips were buzzing when she pulled back.

He looked stunned, and more than a bit suspicious. Not that she blamed him. The last time she'd initiated anything, she'd knocked him out and tied him up. This time, she was startled by the heat that warmed her cheeks at such a brief touch.

"Move to the back of the compartment," Zaria said, waving at Kos as she stepped closer to the clear wall. "I don't have to remind you what can happen if you try anything, do I?"

Kos didn't reply but he did take a few steps back, his eyes never leaving Hope.

When Zaria seemed satisfied, she touched a button on her belt and the clear wall fronting the cell slid open. Hope stepped through it and watched as it closed behind her just as quickly, the wall locking into place. So, the door was activated externally, thought Hope. She wondered how many others could open doors with a button on their belt, and she tried to remember which button Zaria had touched. The belt she wore was studded with gold buttons, and she suspected each one did something different on the ship.

Zaria grabbed her by the elbow, jerking her forward roughly and propelling her down the spiraling ramp. The lights were on now, and once again, she could see inside the clear compartments that lined the way, although now that she was a resident of a cell herself, she made a point of *not* looking inside as they passed.

"So," she said, after they'd wound their way down almost to the bottom. "I take it the beauty parlor is in the basement?"

Hope didn't know why she made the stupid joke. Maybe to show Zaria she wasn't scared, even though her legs were shaking?

The alien glanced over at her, then a menacing smile spread across her face. "Is that what you call it on your home world? The place where females go to be altered?"

"I guess," Hope said, regretting opening her mouth.

They reached a set of double doors that weren't transparent. When they paused in front, they swished open. Hope felt all sense of courage or levity drain out of her body, and she went cold.

The room looked nothing like a hair salon or beauty parlor, or any kind of place Hope had ever seen where women went to get fixed up. With lots of shiny chrome tables and aliens in what appeared to be white lab gowns and face masks, it looked more like a medical research facility. What the hell kind of things were they planning on doing to her anyway? She started to back away as several of the masked faces swiveled toward her.

Zaria nudged her through the doors with a sharp tug, then leaned close to Hope's ear. "I have a feeling this is not going to be very much like your 'beauty parlors.'"

She gulped. She had a feeling Zaria was right.

CHAPTER
SEVENTEEN

K os paced back and forth in the cell. She'd been gone too long. He crossed to the clear front and slammed his palm against the surface. "Anyone out there?"

The cells were not soundproof, and he could hear noises throughout the ship. They were preparing for the party, and every so often a burly member of the Curator's staff would walk by carrying a crate or box. Loud clanging and banging punctuated the usual quiet, and a faint flowery scent wafted through the air. Several times already, the lights in the ship had changed color and he wondered if they were testing them out.

There were now a pair of small, high metal tables perched outside their cell as well as a cluster of stools. If he hadn't felt like an exhibit before, he did now.

"They won't hurt her," the neighboring alien said from where she sat curled up on the floor. He remembered that her name was Xarla.

"How can you be sure?" He turned away from the wall to meet her eyes.

"They never damage the collection. The Curator wouldn't allow it." Xarla gave him a weak smile. "She might look a bit different when she returns, though."

"Why haven't they taken you yet?" Kos asked.

She let out a small, fluttery laugh. "I'm not the main attraction. Besides, my performance doesn't require it. I'm surprised they haven't removed you to be prepped, although the Curator might already think you look impressive enough in your Drexian clothes."

Kos tried to ignore the uneasy feeling in his gut as he glanced down at the dark pants and shirt. It had certainly looked better, but now wasn't the time to worry about protocol. It wasn't like he was wearing a formal uniform jacket or his decorated sash.

Zaria strode into view outside the clear wall, and Xarla slunk back deeper into her own compartment. Kos refused to be intimidated by the alien with crimson skin, even though the sight of her made him want to shudder.

"Back away from the barrier, Drexian," the Curator's enforcer said as she swung her long tresses off her shoulder.

"Where is the human?" he asked, not making a move.

Zaria rolled her eyes. "Your precious female is fine, although I don't know what you Drexians see in them. They're so small and fragile."

Kos tamped down a surge of fury he felt building in his chest. "If you harm so much as a hair on her—"

"Relax, Drexian. Why would we want to hurt her?" Zaria grinned and looked even more terrifying. "The Curator is insistent that his performers be healthy. Makes for a better show."

Kos clenched his jaw and his teeth ground together. "Then why has she been gone—?"

Zaria waved a hand to cut him off. "You'll get her back, but now I need you to back away from the front so I can get *you* ready."

Kos still didn't move. "Me? But I thought—"

"Yeah, we don't need you to think, Drexian." She narrowed her eyes and pulled a laser whip from her belt. "Move back."

Kos grunted his displeasure but took a few steps back as Zaria pressed her belt and the clear door slid open. She snapped the whip as she stepped inside.

Kos sized up his odds quickly. He could probably get the jump on her, even if it meant getting caught by the whip. But he didn't know where they'd taken Hope, and no way was he escaping without her.

"Take off your shirt," Zaria said, flicking the whip so that it made a sizzling sound.

He stared at her, and the alien sighed. "I thought your kind was supposed to be smart. Don't tell me you're all brawn and no brains."

Kos's fingers tingled with the desire to snatch the whip from her hand, but he reminded himself to keep his cool. He pulled the shirt over his head in a single, swift movement, tossing it so Zaria had to raise an arm over her head to catch it.

Her eyes flicked across his bare chest, her black pupils dilating slightly. Her tongue wet her bottom lip, which quirked up in a half smile, as she folded the shirt over one arm. "Now the pants."

Kos refused to let her see his anger, dropping his pants briskly around his ankles and kicking them over to her without a word.

Zaria's sly smile grew as she appraised him. "I see it's true what they say about Drexians. You are big all over."

Kos met her gaze without flinching. If she thought she would intimidate him, she was wrong. Even if he was standing in nothing but his tight, black boxer-briefs.

"Now, that's better," Zaria said. "That clothing covered too much flesh, don't you think?"

Kos didn't answer, although he now noticed something dark draped over her other arm. She followed his gaze. "Look familiar?"

It did not, but he caught it when she tossed it at him, holding up the dark garment and realizing that the uneven strips of leather made up a skirt of some kind. His throat constricted when he saw the metal flame pinned to one side.

"You may be our first Drexian, but that doesn't mean the

Curator has not been preparing for the time when he would host one of your kind."

"This is..." Kos's words died on his lips.

"What Drexian warriors wore in battle a millennium ago," Zaria said. "Before you left your home world and became the police of the galaxy."

Kos turned the garment over in his hands. He'd never worn a traditional Drexian kilt, but he'd heard of them. Made from animal skins, his Drexian ancestors had worn them bare-chested, with leather belts ringing their waists to hold their curved blades. His people still used curved blades, when they weren't firing blasters, but Inferno Force was the only division of their military that had retained the flame insignia all Drexians used to wear on their battle kilts. Seeing this garment made him both proud to be a Drexian and disgusted that his first experience wearing the traditional battle garb would be as a captive of the Curator.

Zaria snapped her whip to get his attention, and Kos numbly stepped into it, fastening the kilt so it sat slightly below his waist.

"Mmmm." Zaria practically purred as she looked at him. "I prefer you like this, Drexian—rough and primal. Let's just hope your little human isn't too terrified when she sees you."

She laughed as she backed out, closing the transparent barrier behind her. When she'd disappeared down the ramp, Xarla emerged from the back of her cell. "Is that really what your people wear? It's very different from what you had on."

"We did a long time ago," Kos told her, glancing down at the black leather that hung from his waist and only reached mid-thigh. "But we evolved and modernized."

Xarla's eyes were wide. "I can see that."

The lights flickered before dimming, and Kos spun around. "What's going on now?"

Zaria sighed. "The Curator likes us to be rested before the guests arrive. If I were you, I'd sleep some. Once the party starts, there are no breaks."

Kos stalked over to the bed and flopped down on it, lacing his fingers behind his head and staring up at the ceiling. It had been hours, and he'd made zero headway in finding a way out. The cells seemed impenetrable; the only way out was activating the button on one of the crew members' belts. Something he couldn't do from inside.

A swish made him sit up quickly. Hope walked back in, and his throat tightened when he saw her.

Instead of the utilitarian outfit she'd been wearing, she was now in a dress that looked like liquid gold. The shimmery fabric was nearly transparent, draping from one shoulder and cinching at the waist before falling to the floor with a slit up one thigh. Her bare skin—and there was plenty of it—also appeared to shimmer, flecks of gold catching in the low light. Her pale hair fell in waves down her shoulders and her face had been dramatically made up, with black lines sweeping out from the corners of her eyes.

She paused as the clear wall slid shut behind her.

He stood, his mouth dry as he tried to speak. "You're okay?"

She nodded but walked forward gingerly. "I was out for most of it, but I'm pretty sure they ripped every hair off my body."

His gaze went to her head.

"Not there, but everywhere else."

"Oh." He did not know much about human females, but he had not thought them to be hairy. "Is that all?"

She shot him a look. "Well, they covered me with some sort of sparkly lotion, and then they made me look like a drag queen."

Kos cocked his head. "Is this a type of Earth royalty?"

She snorted a laugh. "Not exactly." She studied him. "So, aside from dressing you like Conan, they didn't do anything to you?"

"No," he admitted.

"Typical," she muttered.

"You do not find this too scary?" he asked, glancing down at his Drexian battle kilt.

Hope shook her head. "I mean, it's nice that you're showing

more leg than me. I would have been pissed if you'd gotten to wear your uniform." She passed him and flopped onto the bed. "I still feel a little bit drowsy from whatever they gave me."

"You should sleep," he said. "Xarla says there are no breaks during the parties."

Hope propped herself up on her elbows and looked at him. "That goes for you too. We can't exactly stage a prison break if you're exhausted."

He lowered himself onto the bed next to her, trying not to let his eyes wander to the expanse of bare leg or to her hard nipples poking against the sheer fabric. The dress left almost nothing to the imagination, so he closed his eyes as he lay on his back, willing his cock to stop throbbing.

After a few moments of feeling her shift restlessly next to him, he opened his eyes. "What is wrong?"

"You mean aside from being held prisoner by the universe's creepiest alien and being forced to take part in some messed-up sex party?" she asked. "Oh, nothing I guess."

He turned to look at her in the near dark. "You are scared?"

"More like freaked out. Aren't you?"

"I am worried for you, not for myself," Kos said. "If anyone tries to touch you or hurt you, I will have to fight them."

"But you can't." She turned and touched a hand to his arm. "They'll kill you."

"I will defend you with my life, even if that means dying," he said. "But I would not want to leave you alone."

"I don't want that either." Her voice cracked. "Any of it."

He turned his head back so that he stared at the ceiling. "Then let us hope no one tries to touch you tonight."

Kos felt the warmth of her body and heard the soft swish of the fabric as she moved closer to him, and his breath caught in his throat when she straddled him.

"What are you doing?" He could see the outline of her as she leaned over, brushing her lips against his.

"If this is going to happen, it's going to happen *my* way."

His heart pounded as her soft curls fell to either side of her face, creating a curtain around them. "I do not understand."

Her mouth moved to his ear, and she nipped it before sucking on the lobe. He bit back a groan.

"I told you, big guy," she said, her breathy voice sending jolts down his spine. "It's not that I don't want to fuck you. I'm just not crazy about doing it with an audience, especially not the first time."

His cock pulsed, straining in his boxer briefs as she ground her body against it. "You want to... Now?"

She pulled back slightly, her breathing heavy. "Unless you don't want me."

"I want you," he said, almost too quickly, his hand tangling in her curls. "I've wanted you since I first laid eyes on you on that pirate ship. I knew in that moment that you were mine."

"Looks like you're going to get to show me just how much I'm yours, big guy," she whispered.

Kos felt the desire storm through him as she swiveled her hips again and rubbed against his cock. All his anger and frustration transformed instantly into a blinding need. Fisting his hand in her hair, he yanked her mouth to his, parting her lips with a dominant sweep of his tongue. Her body seemed to melt against him, and she moaned in his mouth.

Kos looped a hand around her waist and flipped her onto her back without breaking the kiss. When he was between her legs, he tore his mouth from hers, seeing her eyes flare with surprise and then her own desire.

This was not how he had envisioned taking his mate for the first time, but she was right. This would be theirs alone. He would share this with nobody. He would never share her. Hope was his. Always.

CHAPTER

EIGHTEEN

Hope lay underneath him, her heart thundering in her chest. His body was warm, and she ran her hands across the bare expanse of his back. When her fingertips brushed up against the bumps running down his spine, he let out a low rumble.

She hadn't had much time to explore his nodes before—back on the ship, she'd been concentrating on seducing him so she could knock him out—and now she savored the feel of them. "I like these," she whispered.

Kos arched his back, and Hope bumped her fingers down his spine, the nodes hot and hard. She circled each one before moving on to the next, loving how they warmed under her strokes.

His breathing was labored as he braced his body with his elbows so he wouldn't crush her. "I like the way you touch them. I like the way you touch me."

Now that Kos was wearing nothing but a dark kilt, there was more of him to touch, and she couldn't stop her hands from roaming across his broad muscles. She brought one hand around to his stomach, which was a hard row of corded muscles. Hearing her own sharp inhalation, she dragged her fingers lower and traced the ridged muscle that formed a V.

Holy shit. How did he get this body by being first officer of a space station? This was not the physique you got doing a desk job. Her breath stuttered in her chest as she felt the hard bar of his cock swell between her legs.

Her pulse fluttered. Why did she feel nervous? Her gaze darted to the side and scanned the room. Sure, they were in a glass cage, but it was pretty dark, and no one was watching. The cell to one side of them was empty, and Xarla had done a good job of making herself scarce.

It wasn't like she was some innocent virgin. She'd been with her share of men; sex had always been something normal and healthy to her—and purely for fun. Then why did this feel so different? Why did Kos feel different?

His breath was warm against her neck as he leaned down and kissed a trail from her earlobe to her lips, capturing her mouth and kissing her deeply. Her head swam as their tongues swirled, and when he pulled away, she felt drugged.

It was different because Kos was different. He wasn't like every other guy she'd hooked up with. Even though the whole mate-for-life, tribute bride concept freaked her out, she knew Kos would protect her with his life. He would never ditch her. Maybe that was what scared her the most.

"Hope?" His furtive whisper jerked her out of her thoughts.

"Sorry," she said. "Did you ask me something?"

He cupped her chin in one hand. "Are you sure?"

She smiled at him, even as she felt dazed from his kisses. Even as his entire body shook with desire, he was still worrying about her.

Hope nodded. "I'm sure."

She was sure. She knew she probably shouldn't want to sleep with the guy who was convinced she was going to marry him—wasn't this leading him on in the worst kind of way?—but if this was going to happen, it was going to happen on her terms.

She dragged a hand through his hair and then scratched her nails down the back of his neck. "Do you want me to beg you?"

He growled low as he crushed his mouth to hers, and she felt the air leave her. He moved his hand up one leg, pushing aside the fabric of her dress, and she hooked the freed leg around his waist.

Doing the same with the fabric of his kilt, Hope tugged at his snug underwear. His moans became louder in her mouth, and he kissed her like he was starved for her taste as she rocked into him, feeling his hard length as it sprung free from the tight fabric.

He tore his mouth from hers, his eyes wild and his breaths jagged pants. "*Grek.*" He moved his mouth down her jaw until he reached one pebbled nipple, tugging aside the fabric and exposing it to the air.

Hope dug her fingers into his shoulders as he started to lick, a breathless groan escaping her lips. Heat rushed between her thighs, and she writhed restlessly as he switched his hot mouth to the other breast, sucking the nipple deep into his mouth.

"Kos," she managed to whisper, her hands grasping his bare shoulders. Her anxiety had melted away. She was no longer nervous. She wanted him, and she didn't care what it meant. She'd never felt such a primal desire for another person.

He glanced up at her, and she could see the barest flash of a smile as he moved down further, pushing her thighs apart. Hope sucked in a sharp breath as the heat of his tongue spread her folds, her fingernails digging into his flesh. When he found her clit and began circling it with the tip of his tongue, she bit her bottom lip to keep from crying out.

Hope wished she could watch him, but being in the dark as the sensations rocketed through her body was incredibly sexy. Her eyelids fluttered closed as his movements sped up, his tongue flicking her rapidly then returning to slow circles. He slid his thick hands around her ass and lifted her hips, spreading her legs open even more for him. She gyrated her hips as his tongue sent shivers of pleasure through her, and soon she was arching up as her body quivered.

"Come for me," he ordered, his voice a dark purr.

She didn't want anyone to hear her, so she bit down on her bottom lip at the same time Kos slid one of his thick fingers inside her. He continued flicking her clit as he stroked his finger in and out, then he added a second finger and a gasp escaped her lips. If she was this full with just his fingers…

He slowed his pace, lapping at her and making her hips twitch with need.

"More," she whispered.

He gave her more, sucking hard on her clit again, his fingers lodging deep. She bucked up, biting back a strangled cry as she spasmed around him and then went limp.

Hope saw him sit back, the silhouette of his cock jutting out from his body as he looked down at her. Even though her skin still tingled from his touch, she sat up and reached for him.

His cock felt even bigger than it looked, and her hand didn't close as she grasped the base. He released a breath as she moved her hand up and down his thick shaft, and then he let out what she assumed was a Drexian curse.

A flush of possessive pleasure rushed through her—a surprise, since she'd never felt any sort of ownership over any man before. But as she fisted his huge cock and heard his breathing quicken, Hope felt an overwhelming desire to stake her claim on him.

Looking up and catching his eyes, she brought her lips to the tip of his cock. His eyes grew wide, and he stopped breathing as she swirled her tongue around his crown, tasting the salty slickness.

He tangled one hand in her hair. "Gods, Hope."

The ragged desire in his voice was all she needed to hear. She sucked the head of his cock into her mouth and felt his grip on her hair tighten. She took him as deep as she could, sucking hard and tightening her throat even though she couldn't take all of him. He was too big, and the thought of how good that thick cock would feel inside her made her moan. She didn't even care who heard her.

She moved back up his length, swirling around his crown again, but before she could take him deep again, Kos had pushed her back onto the bed

"Hey," she protested softly. "I wasn't done."

"As good as your mouth feels, *cinnara*, I have waited long enough to be inside you." He knelt between her legs and pushed them open further.

Hope let her legs fall open, wanting him inside her, needing him. "Then don't wait, big guy."

He jerked her hips to him, notching his cock at her entrance. "You are mine. Whatever happens, you will always be mine."

Before she could think about it, she was nodding. Something about being in that place made her want to be his. She wanted to be claimed by him. Wanted to be the Drexian's mate, as if the act of being claimed by the warrior would protect her. "I'm all yours, Kos."

He pressed the thick head of his cock inside, and she drew a quick breath. Even that slight movement stretched her, and she instinctively shifted back.

Kos grasped her hips to stop her. "You can take me, *cinnara*. I know you can. You're meant to be mine."

She didn't know what 'cinnara' meant, but the word sent a wave of pleasure through her. "I want to. I want to feel all of you."

He growled low, holding her steady as he pressed deeper into her, and she felt him stretch her more than she'd ever been stretched. She'd never been so full, and when he'd buried himself to the hilt, she allowed herself to breathe again.

"So tight," he gasped, holding himself inside her.

She moved her hips as her body adjusted, feeling him embedded so deep her eyes almost rolled up into the back of her head.

"I knew you would feel this way," he murmured as he lowered himself so that their bodies were flush. "So perfect."

Kos dragged himself part of the way out before thrusting back in, making Hope emit a small breathy sound. She wrapped her arms around him, digging her nails into the muscles of his back.

"More," she whispered in his ear.

He began to move faster, and she clutched at his slick shoulders as he stroked deep. She wanted to moan and scream, but she forced herself to stay quiet. The only sound was that of their mingled panting as she circled his waist with her legs.

CHAPTER
NINETEEN

G*rek,* he'd never felt anything like it. He'd never felt anything like her.

He plunged into her again until he was fully seated inside, the squeeze of her tight heat almost making him blind with desire.

Even in the dim light, he could see that her brown eyes were half-lidded, and her mouth opened wider with each thrust. "Kos."

He nestled his head next to her ear. "Yes, *cinnara*?" He drew himself out and thrust deeper. "Is this what you wanted?"

Her response was a half murmur, half whimper, and her soft sounds drove him even wilder. As it was, he could barely control himself, driving deep and working himself between her thighs.

He'd waited so long for her. So long for a female who would be only his. He'd lost her, searched for her, fought for her. Now, she was with him. Finally surrendering herself to him. And the thought almost drove him over the edge.

He leaned close to her, his body hovering over hers and their heat mingling. His hips moved fast as he drove into her again and again, her rapid breaths spurring him on.

"You feel so good," she whispered, pulling his head down so that her lips buzzed his ear. "Feels so right being filled by you."

He stifled a roar that was building in his chest. He wanted to bellow his pleasure, but he also wanted to keep her to himself. He wanted to keep her tight heat and her breathy noises all for himself.

They may be trapped in a bizarre prison, but they were together, and he would find a way to get them out. Until that time, he would stake his claim on her, so there was no doubt the human female was his and his alone. No one else would touch her. No one else would fuck her. She was his. His mate.

A growl escaped his lips, and he drowned it by crushing his mouth to hers, feeling her lips part willingly and let him in. The sweet taste of her made him wild with desire, and he pounded into her even faster, swallowing her cries.

Her legs tightened around his waist as they started to shake. He felt her body flutter around his cock and then clamp down on him. Hope arched her back, her hands clawing at his back and scoring his flesh. The pain was nothing compared to the ecstasy of her body quivering around his cock. Nothing had ever felt as good or as perfect as she did coming with him inside her.

She ripped her mouth from his, letting out a desperate gasp and whispering his name. "Kos."

Hearing his name on her lips made his thrusts fast and desperate, pistoning into his mate before he knifed up, thrusting hard inside her and holding himself deep as he threw his head back in silent release.

When he collapsed on top of her and rolled off to the side so as not to crush her, Hope rolled with him, lying splayed across his chest and breathing hard.

"Wow," she managed between shallow breaths. "Are all Drexians like that?"

He laughed softly. "I do not know."

She traced a finger down his chest, which was slick with sweat.

"If you are, I know why you don't have a mass revolt of the tribute brides."

"Does that mean you would like more?"

Hope crawled on top of him, shifting herself down so that his still-hard cock bumped against her opening. She raised herself slightly, angling her hips and taking him inside her again, letting out a breath as she sat up all the way and took him deep. "I don't know if I'm ever going to get enough of this."

He felt the same way, his eyelids fluttering as her snug warmth enveloped his cock.

"My *cinnara*," he whispered, stroking his hands down her back and cupping her bare ass cheeks. He lifted her up and then drove her back down, savoring the sharp gasp as she was impaled on his cock. "Only mine."

CHAPTER
TWENTY

"Are you nervous?" Xarla asked, smoothing her hands down the front of her thighs.

The lights had been turned on again, although not to full illumination. The lighting was still dim, but alternated with colored, patterned lights that danced across the ramp outside their compartments. Even inside the cells, the light was colored. Xarla's cell glowed a pale blue, while the room that Hope and Kos were in glowed gold.

Instrumental music filled the air and only now were voices beginning to drift up from the bottom of the ship. The laughter was interspersed with the clink of glasses, letting Hope know the party had officially begun.

"Nervous?" Hope asked, eyeing the hallway outside the cells. "Well, I've never been to a sex party before, so I guess you could say I'm a little nervous."

"You get used to it," the alien told her, even though she worked her own hands nervously.

Hope glanced at the small table that had been wheeled in earlier and swallowed hard. Aside from tall cylinders of water, it held several bottles of alien bubbly along with a bowl of glistening fruit that reminded Hope of strawberries. If strawberries were purple and completely round.

It didn't take a genius to know that the fruit and bubbly were supposed to be part of their act, which made her want to refuse them on principle. Although, getting totally drunk probably wouldn't be the worst way to get through the night.

She looked over at Kos as he paced a small circle behind the bed. If it was possible, he seemed more wired. The Drexian who'd whispered sweetly in her ear while he was inside her had gone, replaced by the Drexian pounding across the floor, his eyes burning with fury.

She walked over and put a hand on his arm. "I don't think you pacing a hole in the floor will do much."

He stopped and shot a look at her, before seeming to remember who she was. His expression relaxed, and he placed a hand over hers. "I am sorry, *cinnara*. I am trying to think of a way to escape."

"Any luck?" She tried to smile, but she knew her attempt was weak.

His only response was to take her face in his hand and drag a thumb across her bottom lip. "I can't stand the thought of..." He shook his head, his gray eyes darkening. "I will not let these creatures dishonor you."

His touch sent jolts through her. "I appreciate the whole Drexian honor thing, but at this point I think we need to focus on survival. If you get killed trying to defend my honor, where would that leave me?"

He pressed his lips together and shut his eyes for a moment. "You are right. The most important thing is getting you out of here."

"I've seen you battle a pretty scary-looking pirate, so if anyone can do it, my money is on you."

He kissed her softly, and she let herself sink into him, forgetting her surroundings for a moment. That is until she heard Xarla clear her throat loudly.

Hope twisted around and saw that the party had moved up.

Guests in elaborate gowns and brightly colored suits were walking outside their cells and peering inside unabashedly.

Why wouldn't they? They were the type of aliens who would pay handsomely to attend a creepy sex party aboard an illegal prison. She doubted shame was part of their repertoire.

Glancing over at Xarla, she saw that the alien had begun a slow dance that was much more erotic than the version she'd shown earlier. A couple in matching green gowns with tall headdresses on their cone-shaped heads stood transfixed, clapping when Xarla tucked her head behind her own ass and swished her tail in a circle.

Kos's hand tightened on her face, and he used his other arm to pull her closer. "Don't look at any of that. Keep your eyes on me."

Easier said than done, she thought. Hope heard voices outside their cell, the words "Drexian" and "human" floating through the air. She looked up at Kos and focused on his gaze, which was locked onto hers. She could almost lose herself in the soft gray of his eyes and the warmth of his body next to hers.

A hard tap on the glass made her jump. Almost.

"Don't turn," Kos said, his gaze flitting over her head for the briefest of moments before returning to her.

She nodded, even as she heard raised voices outside.

A muscle in Kos's jaw ticked, but he stroked her cheek with one finger. Without breaking his gaze, he lowered his mouth to hers, kissing her gently at first and then parting her lips and delving deeper.

Hope put a hand on his bare chest to brace herself as he wrapped an arm around her back and pressed himself against her. The loud voices turned to cheers, and her body stiffened. She pulled away, even though she instantly regretted it.

She was plunged back into reality, and she was very aware of more party guests gathered outside their glass. She knew she shouldn't look, but she was too curious. Twisting her neck, she saw a strange assortment of aliens watching her. Drinks in hand, some were watching her and Kos with undisguised lust while others were talking to each other as if nothing unusual was going on.

Her heart beat erratically, and her palms were damp. She turned back to Kos and rested her forehead on his chest. "I can't do this."

He circled his thick arms around her and tucked her head under his chin, kissing the top of her head. "It's okay, *cinnara*."

She took a deep breath, trying to block out the voices growing louder outside the glass. "What does that mean, *cinnara*?"

"It's Drexian for 'my love.'"

Usually, that type of term of endearment would send her running or packing, but now it only sent warmth through her entire body. She traced her fingers across the hard curves of his chest muscles and watched his nipple harden in response.

"Sorry," she murmured with a small giggle.

"You never have to apologize for touching me," he said, his voice low so only she could hear. "I am yours. You may touch me any way you wish."

Pounding on the glass made them both jump.

"Now I know how fish at the aquarium feel," Hope muttered. If she ever got back to Earth, she would never set foot in another zoo or aquarium for as long as she lived.

Back to Earth. Did she even want to go back anymore? She'd been hell-bent on the idea not too long ago, but that was before her stupid obsession had gotten them into their current situation. And it was before she'd slept with Kos.

She gave herself a hard shake. *Come off it, girl. You can't change your life plans after one fuck, even if it was a really great fuck.*

But it hadn't just been another fuck, had it? She flattened her hand across the row of bumpy ridges stretching across his stomach. And it wasn't just that he was incredibly hot, which he was. No, there was something more. Something she'd never felt before.

The little voice in the back of her head nagged at her, reminding her that people were all the same. They all left, one way or another.

She peered up at Kos. But he hadn't ditched her, even when she'd seriously deserved it. He was still right by her side.

"Well, isn't this sweet? And boring."

The voice was so close it made Hope whip her head around. Zaria stood inside the compartment, her laser whip humming by her side. Somehow she'd managed to open the door and come inside without them hearing, although that wasn't a huge shock, considering the music and loud voices made it hard to hear much.

Kos spun Hope behind him, putting himself between her and the alien with the whip. "What do you want?"

Zaria leaned forward, her words a near hiss. "I want you to do what you're supposed to do." She snapped the whip, and the end sizzled. "Or I'll give our guests another kind of show to watch."

"Go ahead," Kos said. "Pain doesn't frighten me."

Zaria grinned, advancing on Kos, and Hope knew she was going to enjoy whatever punishment she was about to mete out.

"Stop!" She stepped in front of Kos and held out her hands. "You don't need to do that. We'll...do what you want."

Zaria's lips curled up in a cold smile. "Now that's more like it." Her gaze flicked between Hope and Kos. "See that you do."

She spun on her heel and stalked out. Hope noticed several of the guests outside looked genuinely disappointed that they weren't going to see Kos get whipped.

"You didn't need to do that," Kos said, when she turned around. "I told you I would protect you."

Hope took him by the hand and led him to the edge of the bed. She pushed him down so he was sitting on the end, and then lowered herself so that she straddled his lap. His eyes flared with surprise and desire, but he shook his head. "I told you that you wouldn't have to—"

She put a finger over his lips. "I know. But now it's my turn to protect you."

CHAPTER
TWENTY-ONE

K os gaped up at Hope. "Protect me?"

Her back was to the glass, but he could see the growing crowd over her shoulder. The colored lights swirled across the faces of the aliens watching them, contorting their already manic expressions. Spirals of purple and pink danced over the garishly hued robes and intricately styled hair, making the spectators appear to morph. The clear walls blocked out enough of the noise that he couldn't make out exact words, but he could hear the jeers and catcalls over the increasingly intense thump of the music.

She leaned over so that her lips were against his ear, her hair falling onto his shoulder and tickling his bare skin. "The best way to keep them happy is to give them what they want. More than what they want."

He bristled at her words, even though the buzz of her lips sent an involuntary shiver down his back and made his nodes pulse. He knew she was right, but he didn't like it.

Hope took his earlobe between her lips and sucked gently, making more than just his nodes throb. She nipped at it hard, and he jerked back, seeing the challenge in her eyes.

"Spank me," she told him.

"What?" He must have heard her wrong over the cacophony of noise.

She wiggled her ass on his lap. "You heard me. I told you to spank me." When she saw his hesitation, she added, "They'll love it, and it'll buy us some time."

His female was as clever as she was beautiful, he thought. There was more than one way to satisfy a crowd who'd come to be scandalized and aroused.

He cocked his head as she braced her hands on his shoulders. "Only because you asked me to."

He slapped her ass, and she let out a yelp much louder than the slap deserved.

"Come on, big guy," she told him, a smile playing at the corner of her mouth. "I know you can hit harder than that, and I know you must want to."

"Why would I want to?"

She shrugged. "Don't you want to give me a spanking for me being a dip shit and getting us into this mess?"

He slapped her ass again, but this time harder. "You make a good point, *cinnara*."

Her eyes flared. "That hurt. You don't have to put on *that* good of a show."

He could see out of the corner of his eye that the party guests were cheering. He slapped her other ass cheek this time and felt the flesh quiver under his palm.

"Son of a..." she said, trying to wiggle off him.

He clamped his hands on the sides of her hips to keep her on his lap and pulled her close enough so that his head was beside hers. "You were right. They love it."

"And I think you're loving it a little too much," she said.

"You were correct," he whispered in her ear. "You do deserve punishment for tricking me and knocking me out."

"I thought you forgave me," she said.

"I did," Kos told her. "But as your Drexian mate, it's my responsibility to ensure that you learn from your mistakes. And it's my right to keep you in line."

"Keep me in line?" Hope spluttered.

Kos pulled her into a forceful kiss, his mouth opening hers and his tongue fighting with hers as he pinned her arms behind her and held her wrists together with one large hand.

"Are you taking the piss?" she said, jerking her mouth from his.

He lifted her in one swift motion and flipped her over his knees, his hand still holding her wrists together at the small of her back. Hope struggled and thrashed as he held her. The crowd cheered, waving their arms and clapping wildly.

Hope craned her neck around to meet his eyes. "I swear, I'm going to beat the ever-loving shit out of you for this."

He leaned down, dodging her head as she attempted to head-butt him. "This was your idea, *cinnara,* and it's working."

She stopped glaring at him and cut her eyes to the crowd, then looked back at him, her eyes narrowed. "Fine, let's do this, but stop enjoying it so much."

He smiled at her, his gaze wandering to her round ass cheeks visible through the sheer fabric of her dress. "I will try, but your ass is just too pretty."

She struggled again, and he groaned as her ass wiggled. He slapped one cheek and got a sharp yelp as a reward. The crowd surged, screaming for more.

Kos's cock throbbed as the female—his mate—lay across his lap, her ass in the air and her arms pinned behind her. Her skin was pink from his smacks, and he was grateful the aliens had taken her underwear. He loved seeing her flushed ass cheeks through the nearly transparent fabric of her dress.

Hope was right. He was enjoying this much more than he would have expected, her noises of protest and struggling arousing him so much, he was grateful she was covering his rock-hard erection.

He was so distracted by his arousal that he loosened his grip on her wrists, and she jerked away, scampering out of his lap and across the bed. He instinctively lunged for her, but she slipped off the bed and danced out of his reach.

The crowd at the glass had grown in size, and even Xarla next door had stopped her acrobatic performance to watch in fascination as Kos chased Hope and pinned her against the wall between their two cells.

Her back was to the wall, and he pressed both her arms over her head. Her eyes were wild, and her cheeks crimson, and she seemed to be just as turned on as he was, the hard points of her nipples straining against the gossamer fabric of her dress.

Kos crushed his mouth to hers, kissing her so hard her head was pressed back against the clear wall. He was lightheaded with desire, the cheers of the spectators dissolving into the background. The only thing he was aware of was the pounding of his blood in his ears and Hope's needy moans in his mouth. When she lifted one leg and hooked it around his hip, grinding into the stiff bar of his cock, Kos growled and pressed himself into her even harder.

A gasp from the next cell made him rear back, the swirling colors and deafening sounds coming back into focus. He stared down at Hope, her lips swollen from his kisses. Her breath hitched in her chest as she looked up at him.

He steadied his breathing. He'd almost gone over the edge and taken her with him. He dropped her arms and cupped her face in one hand. "Do you trust me, *cinnara*?"

She held his gaze. "After the spanking you just gave me, I probably shouldn't."

He moved one hand down and caressed her ass. "I promise there will be no more spanking."

"I trust you," she finally said.

"At least no more spanking from me," he said.

Hope's mouth dangled open. "What?"

"Trust me," he said, kissing her again quickly. "It's our way out of here."

She darted a glance behind him. "I don't know why *you* getting spanked can't be part of the escape plan."

"My ass isn't as round and perfect as yours," Kos said, turning her around so that she faced the wall and pinning her wrists to the small of her back again. "Now just go along with this, and we should be able to make a break for it."

He pivoted to face the crowd that stood nearby on the other side of the glass, rubbing one hand down the curve of her ass and swatting it lightly. Hope shrieked loudly, gyrating her hips as if the blow had been much harder.

"That's my wild mate," he whispered before raising his voice and bellowing over the music, "Who else wants a turn?"

TWENTY-TWO

"What?" She shot daggers at Kos over her shoulder. "This had better work."

If this didn't get them out of there, she was going to kill him.

The music still pounded, the heavy beat seeming to mirror the surging energy of the crowd as they clamored at the clear wall. Seeing the mouths hanging open and the eyes flashing with barely contained desire to inflict pain did not make Hope any happier about Kos's dangerous gambit to escape. If he didn't pull it off, she would be in serious trouble.

She did not see Zaria anywhere. That was good. She doubted the woman would be taken in by the ploy. She did see one of the burly guards from earlier and saw that he seemed just as entranced as the party guests. His pasty gray skin was flushed, and he licked at his lips as he watched through the glass.

"Who will be first?" Kos called out, giving her ass another swat and gaining himself a sharp glare.

A tall alien wearing a shiny indigo suit waving something metallic over his head. "A thousand credits."

Kos leaned close to her ear. "A scream might send the bidding higher."

Hope jerked back, struggling to loosen her arms. "Maybe they'd like to hear you scream, big guy."

Raucous laughter rose up from the spectators.

"Two thousand." An alien wearing yellow robes over a corpulent belly waved his credits in the air. The first bidder scowled but stepped back.

The crowd gasped and cheered as the squat alien stepped forward, pushing them aside with the tip of a silver cane. He handed the shiny discs to the guard, his watery eyes locking on Hope's.

She swallowed down the taste of bile and tried not to shudder. The thought of the doughy creature touching her made her want to puke, but she steadied her breath and reminded herself that Kos was a Drexian warrior trained in battle and strategy. He also had an overdeveloped sense of protectiveness that bordered on obnoxiously chauvinistic, so she knew he wouldn't let anything bad happen to her.

She looked over her shoulder and caught his eyes. "You'd better know what you're doing or I'm going to be seriously fucked off."

"I do," he whispered. "When they open the door to let him in, that's our chance."

Hope looked at the aliens gathered near the clear barrier. How were they going to push their way through all of them? Kos had no weapons and neither of them was dressed to blend in. They'd need to take out the guard and then get past all the other security before they even made it to the hangar bay. Then they'd have to find their ship and manage to get off without being stopped. It seemed impossible.

But what was the alternative? Live their lives trapped inside a kinky prison-like zoo? She'd rather take her chances trying to escape.

Kos's grip on her wrists relaxed, and he held his hand over hers only for show, turning his palm so that it covered her hands. The warmth of his skin sent pulses of heat up her arm, and she managed to give him a half smile.

"By the way, big guy," she said, as the alien in yellow robes negotiated with the guard. "This makes us even. I don't ever want to hear another word about what I did to you. My ass feels like it's on fire."

Kos quirked an eyebrow at her, his gaze drifting to her ass. "Agreed."

They were only a few meters from where the door would slide open, and Hope felt Kos tense as the Curator's guard looked around to see if anyone was watching before he fiddled with the button on his belt.

She would have bet good money that opening the cells during a party wasn't something he was supposed to do alone—or maybe at all—but she also guessed that two thousand credits was probably a lot in alien currency. And no way would the guard be sharing it with anyone else, if the look on his face as he shoved the discs in his pockets was any indication.

"Get ready," Kos whispered out of the corner of his mouth.

She was ready. A noise behind her made her think of Xarla, and she swiveled her head to find the alien who'd been so nice to her. She didn't like the idea of leaving the creature behind. Not when she knew what the rest of Xarla's life would look like as a prisoner of the Curator.

Even though the colorful lights danced across the floor and walls of the neighboring compartment, she couldn't see the willowy alien. Was she hiding, or had she twisted herself into a shape so compact that Hope couldn't spot her?

Shit. She wouldn't even get to say good-bye.

Kos's hand tightened over hers, but he was no longer restraining her; he was grasping her hand. Tearing her gaze away from the next-door cell, she glanced over at the Drexian and her mouth went dry.

She knew Kos was a Drexian, and that the Drexians were known throughout the galaxy as great warriors, but seeing Kos bare chested and wearing only the dark battle kilt really brought it home. The lights bounced over his glistening chest, and the muscles rippling across his back made him look exactly like the deadly warrior he was. His jaw was set in a fierce line as he stood coiled, the energy practically radiating off his huge body. Hope shifted her small hand within the grip of his bigger one, glad the guy was on her side.

Kos flicked his gaze to her briefly, but it was long enough for her to see the determination in his eyes. Determination and a flash of something else for her. Something more than desire and possession. Something tender that made her throat tighten.

She wanted to say something in case everything went to hell, but there was no time. The door slid open and the short alien waddled through the opening, his smile almost manic.

Kos did not wait. He yanked Hope by the arm, spinning them both around the startled creature and knocking him to his knees. The guard, who'd also stepped inside the cell, was backing up quickly and fumbling with his belt.

Panic rose in Hope's chest. They weren't going to be fast enough. The guard was almost back in the corridor, his thick finger jamming his waist as the other guests began staggering back as they realized what was happening.

A flash of movement from above made Hope flinch, as Xarla leapt down on top of the guard the second before he made it outside. Her long legs circled his neck like a pretzel, and she held on even as he tried to pull her off, smacking at his hands with sharp slaps of her tail.

Hope peered up. Had Xarla gotten through the opening at the top of the compartment? She must have, even though it looked too narrow for anyone to get through. Then again, the alien was a contortionist, and Hope suspected she was even more talented than she'd let on.

Kos barreled through the aliens clustered around the opening, pulling her to his side as hands reached for them. Even though the guard was distracted—his face an unnatural shade of red as Xarla constricted her legs around his neck—the guests weren't going to make the escape easy. Some were screaming, and others looked enraged at the turn their entertainment had taken.

A female alien with blue spiky hair grabbed at Hope's arm, so Hope cocked her arm back and punched the creature squarely in the nose. Purple liquid spurted from the alien as something in her face cracked.

"That's for thinking people in cages is a party game," Hope said as the woman clutched her gushing nose and wailed.

Kos jerked her forward again, pushing party guests out of the way like they were matchsticks, and they burst through the crowd. Luckily, the music masked the screams and it was hard to tell what were screams of excitement from elsewhere in the ship and what were screams of alarm. She knew that wouldn't last long, though.

"Xarla!" Hope called out, catching the alien's eye as she twisted her head behind her. "Come on!"

The Curator's guard was now purple-faced, his eyes rolled up into the back of his head, and Xarla leapt off him, letting him drop with a thud that shook the floor. She snatched a cloak off a nearby spectator, who goggled at her as she ran past, catching up to Kos with several long strides.

"Thanks for the assist," Kos said as Xarla tossed him the black cloak. He pulled it over his shoulders with one hand, not letting go of Hope with his other.

"You're welcome." Xarla grinned at Hope as the three ran down the corridor, dodging through the crowds who were still unaware that some of the prisoners had escaped. Their attention was too focused on what was happening behind the glass to notice three aliens moving swiftly behind them.

Hope tried not to look inside the cells, reminding herself that they couldn't break everyone out but making a mental pledge that if they got away, she would insist they hunt down the Curator and free everyone. That was, *if* they got away themselves.

They'd almost made it to the bottom of the spiraling corridor when red alarm lighting started to flash. Kos scooped her up without a word and broke into a full-on run.

CHAPTER
TWENTY-THREE

Hope was light in his arms, and Kos pushed himself to run harder than he ever had before as he reached the doors to the hangar bay. They glided open, causing two guards who'd been sitting on either side to jump up. Kos shifted Hope to one side so he could knock out one of the guards with a single hard punch. He spun to take on the other, but Xarla had already leapt up and circled the guard's neck with her legs. Within moments, the guard had dropped to the floor, unconscious.

"You'll have to teach me that," he said, nodding to her in thanks as they hurried across the hangar bay.

Xarla laughed, her emerald eyes flashing. "You have too many bones."

Kos wondered exactly what type of alien Xarla was, but thought he'd wait to ask until they'd escaped. Red alarm lights flashed overhead, more noticeable here than in the rest of the ship, where colored lights were part of the decor. He knew they were losing their head start advantage more every moment.

"Put me down," Hope said, wiggling in his arms. "I can run, you know. Maybe not as fast as you, but I'm not an invalid."

He'd almost forgotten he was carrying her, so he dutifully set her down, then grabbed her by the hand and tugged her behind him. "Less talking, more running."

Spotting their shuttle craft, Kos led them to the far end of the wide space, which was filled with ships, most likely owned by all the guests of the Curator. He wished he had time to sabotage all of them, but his top priority was getting off the ship. Revenge would come later, he promised himself.

There were a few pilots milling about some of the docked ships, but none seemed too interested in them as they made their way to the dark-hulled Drexian shuttle. Thanks to the black cloak, Kos didn't look too out of the ordinary, and, from the way the pilots averted their eyes, he suspected that this wasn't the first time a male had brought two females to a ship during a party.

He quickly assessed the shuttle. It looked untouched, and he could only hope the Curator hadn't thought to disable it in any way. Why would he, Kos thought? The arrogant male would never have expected one of his prisoners to escape.

Touching a palm to the outside panel, Kos waited as the ramp lowered. He glanced behind him but saw no one coming. He hoped they were still assessing what had happened inside the ship. There was enough general chaos in the party that it might take some time to determine who was missing and where they'd gone. Time Kos would not waste.

Before the ramp touched down completely, he ran up with Hope and Xarla behind him. Dropping Hope's hand, he motioned to one of the seats as he rushed to the pilot's chair. "Strap in."

Both females sat quickly—Hope next to him and Xarla behind them—and fastened the safety straps over themselves as he fired up the engines. He tapped his fingers across the console, breathing a sigh of relief when all the lights came on and the engine hummed to life. No damage, and all systems were fully operational.

He checked the stealth shielding system. It was working, which was good. They'd need to use the exclusive Drexian technology if they were going to get away undetected.

As he tapped in a series of commands, the ship rumbled underneath him. He never thought the feel of a ship's engine would be as comforting to him as it was, but he patted the curved edge of the ebony console. "It's good to be back."

"Um, Kos," Hope said, tugging at the sleeve of his cloak. "I think they're onto us."

He cut his eyes to the view out the front of the shuttle, looking to the far left, and his stomach clenched. Zaria had burst through the doors to the hangar bay, accompanied by a handful of guards. One of the guards still looked red-faced from being nearly choked by Xarla.

"They don't look happy," Xarla said, her voice a whisper.

"Good. Those fuckers shouldn't be happy," Hope said, then turned back to him. "Any chance of speeding up the process?"

She looked both defiant and terrified, which he understood completely. He turned his attention back to the console, punching in the final few buttons to get them moving. His stomach churned as he saw Zaria scan the ships and lock her gaze on them.

They'd come this far. No way were they going back, he thought. No way was he going to let any of those aliens ever lay a finger on her.

"Hold on," he said, initiating thrusters and feeling the jolt as the ship rocketed across the open space.

They clipped the pointed wings of a shiny white ship as they roared toward the gaping mouth of the hangar bay, and Kos hoped it was one of the party guests' ships and that they'd taken the wing off entirely. If he'd had time, he would have tried to hit more ships on his way out.

The hard hull of the Drexian ship seemed to be unscathed, and within moments, they burst out of the yawning hangar bay opening. Kos quickly activated the stealth shielding as he banked them hard to one side, curving around the massive cylindrical ship.

Even from outside, he could see flashing colored lights pulsing out the windows, and he choked back his disgust. Kos plotted the

STOLEN

location of the Curator's vessel, even though he suspected the ship rarely stayed in one place for long. At least it would be a place to start when the Drexian hunting party went after him.

Hope released a loud breath. "We did it. We escaped."

As he set a course for the Drexian outpost, he shook his head. "We aren't in the clear yet, although we are invisible."

"So, it's true?" Xarla asked, her voice hushed. "Drexians have invisible ships?"

Kos twisted around to face her. The cat-like alien was peering around the sleek, dark interior of the ship with undisguised wonder. "Not invisible. We have stealth cloaking."

"Which means that other ships can't detect you, right?" Xarla asked.

Kos shrugged. "Right."

"Which is as good as invisible," she said. "We've only heard whispers about the ships that appear out of thin air."

He guessed she was right. Their technology must seem like magic.

Kos glanced over at Hope, whose hands gripped the arm rests of her chair so hard her knuckles were white. She trembled, even though her cheeks were flushed pink. He pulled off his black cloak and draped it over her. "Are you okay?"

She nodded, even though she didn't meet his eyes. "It just hit me how close we came to not getting out of there."

He'd taken rudimentary medic training at the Drexian Academy, but even with his rusty skills, he recognized the symptoms of shock. He put his hands over hers, uncoiling them from the armrests. "Why don't you lie down, *cinnara*?"

She gave a curt shake of her head. "I'm fine. We got away. Everything's going to be fine."

Although her words were reassuring, the tone of her voice—flat and emotionless—was not.

"She doesn't look fine," Xarla said to him under her breath.

119

Kos cut his eyes to his console and then out the front of the ship. Nothing. No ships in pursuit.

He stood and leaned over Hope, unhooking her safety straps. "As captain of this shuttle, I'm ordering you to lie down."

Her eyes focused on him as he picked her up. "So, we're back to you being bossy again? That didn't take long."

He grinned, glad to hear her familiar snark. "And we're back to you complaining about the chain of command again."

"If by chain of command you mean that you get to make all the decisions and I'm supposed to follow your orders, then yep, I'm definitely going to complain about that."

Xarla stifled a laugh, holding a hand over her mouth, as Kos carried Hope to the back of the shuttle. He pressed against one of the hidden panels and a bed popped out of the wall.

"I thought maybe you'd abandoned your stubbornness after everything," he said.

She cocked an eyebrow at him. "If by 'everything', you mean you spanking the shit out of me, then no, that didn't make me any less stubborn."

He set her on the bed, straightening up and putting his hands on his hips. "I thought we called it even."

Her gaze wandered to his bare chest, but then she met his eyes, scrunching her lips together to one side and studying him. "Admit it. The whole spanking thing wasn't just part of the escape plan. You liked it."

"Are you asking if I enjoyed slapping your pretty, round ass and hearing you scream?"

Hope's cheeks reddened, and her pupils flared.

He leaned over, his head next to hers. "Didn't you?"

CHAPTER
TWENTY-FOUR

"Cocky wanker," she said, feeling the corner of her mouth twitching up, even though she fought the smile. No way would she let him know that his spanking her had made her slick between her legs. That would only add fuel to the Drexian's already too-confident fire.

He grinned, like he always did when she used Kiwi slang. "I am not cocky, nor am I a 'wanker.' I am only being honest. Why don't you be honest with me, *cinnara*, and tell me that you liked it?"

She spluttered for a moment, and he laughed. She even heard Xarla attempting not to laugh out loud. "Nothing that happened on that batshit crazy ship should be held against me."

"No?" Kos gave her a crooked grin. "What would you like held against you?"

Hope let out an exaggerated breath. "You're impossible. What I really want is to get out of this ridiculous outfit, forget that any of this happened, and go home."

As soon as the words left her lips, she regretted them. The cockpit went silent, the only sound Xarla's sharp intake of breath. Kos's face darkened and his smile vanished. He stood up straight. "That is what you truly want?"

She gnawed at her lower lip. "I didn't mean for it to come out that way. I just meant—"

"You still want to return home?" he asked. "To Earth?"

Did she? Hope hesitated as she thought. It wasn't like she'd had such a great life on Earth, but it had been hers. For someone who'd been used to going wherever she wanted to go whenever she wanted to, the idea of living in one place for the rest of her life—an alien space station, no less—was a lot to come to terms with.

But if she somehow got back to Earth, she'd never see Kos again. Her heart constricted at the thought. How was it that this alien warrior had managed to get under her skin when no other man ever had? The ache in her heart at the idea of never seeing him again made her want to simultaneously throw her arms around him and run away screaming.

She looked up at him, wanting desperately to give him the answer he wanted, but too scared to give voice to her feelings. Kos stared at her for a moment before his eyes shuttered.

"I suppose I have my answer." He turned and strode back to the pilot's chair, dropping down and facing forward.

Hope's shoulders slumped, and she didn't meet Xarla's eyes when the alien turned to look at her. What was wrong with her? Why couldn't she just admit that she cared about the guy? Why did it feel so impossible to confess to an attachment?

She flopped back on the bed, rolling onto her back and staring up at the black ceiling. The ship's engine hummed steadily, and she knew they were on their way to the Drexian outpost.

And what would happen then? If she and Kos didn't make up, would she end up with the other humans who'd rejected the whole tribute bride concept? Did she want that?

Tears stung the backs of her eyes. She didn't know what she wanted. She just knew that everything had been simpler before she gave a shit about the Drexian who'd sacrificed himself to save her.

And life had been way simpler before she'd been taken off Earth. She'd had no family drama—she hadn't seen her mother in years—

and no husband or boyfriend to complicate her life. The longest relationship she'd ever had had lasted mere weeks, and she couldn't even remember the guy's last name. Mason? Miller? Oh, who cared?

It wasn't like she'd loved the guy. She'd never been in love before, and it had always been a badge she'd worn with honor. Until now.

But it wasn't as if she was in love with Kos. That would be ridiculous. She barely knew him. Sure, they'd had pretty great sex, but that didn't necessarily mean anything, did it?

Hope pressed the heels of her hands over her closed eyes. Then why did she feel a physical ache when she thought about not being with him? Why had the hurt that had crossed his face been like a punch to the gut? She'd broken up with plenty of guys, and she'd never given it much thought.

A tear snaked down the side of her face and she swiped it away. *Get it together, girl. You never cry and certainly not over a guy.*

It must be the shock of everything, she thought. It had been a traumatic few days, after all. Once she was really and truly safe, she'd feel better.

She took a deep breath. She'd be back to her old self soon enough, and she wouldn't feel so weepy. If this was what it felt like to let a guy in—even a little bit—then she'd been right to steer clear. Feeling so out of control and confused was definitely not for her.

Loud static filled the cockpit, and she opened her eyes and twisted around. Xarla had her hands over her ears and Kos tapped quickly at the console until the sound faded.

"We're still too far from Drexian space to get a signal," he said as the cockpit dimmed. "But we need to fly close to Kronock territory to shave some time off our trip. I'm going dark until we're past enemy space."

"Kronock?" Xarla shuddered, wrapping her arms around herself.

"Don't worry," Kos told her. "We're still in stealth mode."

The alien nodded but rubbed her hands briskly over her arms as if trying to warm herself. "The Kronock are the reason my people were scattered across the galaxy. They're the reason my family is gone."

Kos's lips disappeared into a hard white line. "They are the reason many families were destroyed."

Hope slipped off the bed and put a hand on Xarla's shoulder. "Kos won't let us get caught. He's gotten us this far."

He met her eyes for a moment, and she saw a brief flicker of warmth before his expression hardened and he spun back around.

CHAPTER
TWENTY-FIVE

K os focused on the readouts and the star charts displayed in front of him. The steady beep of the computer and the gentle rumble of the engine soothed him, but his heart still raced.

After everything that had happened between them, after everything he had done, she still wanted to leave. He clenched his jaw, trying to understand the female, but finding himself at a loss.

Didn't she understand that she was his mate, and that he would do anything for her? And not only because they'd been matched, but because he'd known she was meant to be his from the second she'd opened her mouth on the pirate ship. The second she'd told the pirate captain to get his fucking hands off her, he'd known. Of course, he should have also known that a female stubborn enough to snap back at an alien large enough to kill her with his bare hands was probably not going to be an easy mate.

He bit back a groan as he thought about how good it had felt to be inside her. How right. He'd never felt as sure about anything in his life as when his cock had been buried inside Hope, and she'd been moaning beneath him.

No, that had been real. At least, it had been for him, and he'd thought it had been for her. He'd been sure of it. Sure that she felt as strongly about him. As sure.

With a brusque shake of his head, he tried to focus on the console. Their course was set, and their speed was steady. Since they were maintaining stealth mode, he couldn't fly as fast as he would have liked to or use jump technology. Even though it would cut days off the journey, it would use too much power and potentially leave them dead in the water. Too risky.

The only thing that mattered was getting them back to the Drexian outpost safely—making sure Hope was safe for good. Even if she didn't want him as a mate.

The thought of returning to the outpost and of Hope joining the reject tributes made his skin go cold. But the thought of her requesting a new match made his jaw clench. It was a rare occurrence, to ask for a new match, but it had happened. Kos knew he wouldn't be able to bear it.

He closed his eyes, trying to push away the mental image of Hope, but it only made it worse. He should have known he didn't deserve her. She was too beautiful, too full of life, too adventurous. She should have been matched with one of the wild warriors from Inferno Force, not him.

You've never been good enough, the little voice in the back of his head reminded him. *You couldn't save Jok'to. You don't deserve her.*

Kos opened his eyes, his vision swimming as he remembered his younger brother. They'd told him it hadn't been his fault, but he'd known better. It should have been him on the ledge when the Kronock fired on the Tarinthian research outpost where his parents had been stationed. It should have been him who'd disappeared as half the mountain had vanished in the explosion. It should have been him who'd saved his younger brother. He was the oldest. He was supposed to protect him. But he hadn't, and nothing anyone had said had ever convinced him that it hadn't been his fault.

Kos swallowed down the lump in his throat. He'd spent so long trying to make up for his failure—working harder than the other officers, putting in more hours, training for longer on the holodecks. But it had still never been enough to redeem him. Not in his mind.

What he didn't want to admit was what he'd feared all along— that Hope deserved someone more worthy than him. Regret roiled in his stomach, and he clenched the edge of the console. Would he ever feel worthy enough?

But if he could not have her, he could not stay while she was matched to another. He didn't think he could stay even if she only chose to live with the rejects.

No, he would have to leave. Maybe he would take the Inferno Force captain up on his offer. Fighting with the rough warriors would be just what he needed. If he could lead the hunting party to track down the Curator, even better. Exacting his revenge in person would be even more sweet.

"Is that normal?" Xarla's voice tore him away from his thoughts.

He followed her extended finger to where it pointed out the front of the ship, his heart sinking when he saw the distant shape growing larger.

Grek. It was a Kronock ship, that he knew, and it seemed to be on an intercept course. The question was, did the enemy know they were there, or was it a coincidence?

Kos quickly altered their course and held his breath. Moments later, the Kronock also changed course to match them.

He let out a long string of Drexian curses he would usually only reserve for his fellow warriors—and only after many drinks.

"What is it?" Hope slipped into the chair next to his, her face pinched with worry. Xarla stood at her side, her hand clutching the top of the black chair.

He thought about lying to the women, but he decided against it. "That's a Kronock ship, and it's on an intercept course."

"Fuck," Hope whispered as Xarla staggered back into her own seat. "Can we outrun it?"

"Not in this shuttle," Kos said, tapping rapidly on the console.

"I'm sending out a distress call on an encrypted Drexian channel. Our only hope is that my people get it in time."

He didn't say what else he was thinking. He would not let the Kronock take them alive.

CHAPTER

TWENTY-SIX

H ope watched as Kos tapped wildly on the shiny console, then twisted her neck to look at Xarla. The alien was white-knuckling her armrests, and her eyes were unfocused, even though she appeared to be staring out the front of the shuttle.

Trying to ignore Kos's muttered curses, she stood from her chair and walked back to join Xarla, taking the seat next to her and closing a hand over the alien's clenched one. "It's going to be okay."

Xarla jerked her head back and forth without meeting her gaze. "You don't know that."

"Maybe not, but I'm pretty sure—"

Xarla swung her head sharply to look at Hope. "You don't know the Kronock."

The expression on the alien's face made the words of comfort Hope had intended to say die on her lips. She felt the tremor in the thin hand underneath hers. "Do you want to talk about what happened?"

Xarla tore her gaze away, peering out the front of the ship again. The tiny spot on the horizon had grown in size, even as Kos changed their course again and the shuttle turned hard to one side. She shook her head, her eyes wide.

Hope had never dealt with loss at the level she suspected Xarla had experienced. It was hard to imagine having your entire planet destroyed and losing everyone you cared about. Hope had gone to pretty extreme lengths to not have many people she'd be upset to lose, but even she felt an ache at the thought of losing everyone. Her mother had been a pretty crappy mother, but she still loved her. It would gut her if she died. And to have Earth decimated? She didn't know if she'd be able to recover and survive half as well as Xarla had.

She focused on the alien woman, who was clearly terrified, and her own stomach churned. How horrible were these Kronock?

Squeezing Xarla's hand, she tried to make her own voice steady. "Kos will do everything possible to save us. Isn't that what Drexians are supposed to do? Keep the galaxy safe?"

Xarla nodded, pulling her gaze away from the view of space. "I know he would do anything to protect you, so I suppose I am lucky to be next to you."

Hope laughed nervously, even though the thought of the Drexian protecting her did make her cheeks warm. "He's going to do everything in his power to keep *all* of us safe."

Kos turned his head quickly, meeting her eyes. For a moment, Hope felt like all the words and hurt between them had vanished, and they were back in the cell on the Curator's ship with the lights out and nobody watching them. Her pulse fluttered at the memory.

When Xarla cleared her throat, Kos pivoted back around, and the connection was gone.

"The Kronock will be within firing range soon," he said, tapping more buttons, the sound of the engines growing louder.

"So, we can shoot at them?" Hope asked.

"This shuttle has limited weaponry."

Hope's stomach sank. "You mean, they'll be able to fire on *us* soon."

He was silent for a moment. "They could easily blow us out of the sky, but that is not my greatest fear."

"What's worse than being blown up?" she asked.

"Being taken prisoner," Xarla said before Kos could.

Hope looked between the two, waiting for an explanation. "I know I'm new to this whole alien war thing, but would someone mind telling me a little more about these Kronock? What's their deal?"

Kos didn't turn to face her as he spoke. "The Kronock are an ancient species—as ancient as the Drexians—but one that was born out of violence. They were a war-like race on their own planet and drove their planet to the brink of collapse with fighting. When they achieved space travel, they immediately began invading other worlds to replenish their own destroyed resources. But they do not understand co-existing, so they pillage a planet and destroy its population, leaving their own kind behind to harvest any resources. It became the mission of the Drexians to stop these invasions and save the other species."

"You did not save mine," Xarla said, her voice soft.

Kos twisted slowly, his eyes cast down. "We were not able to save everyone. The Kronock are widespread, and their warships were a scourge on the galaxy. In some cases, we were too late. We attempted to take in survivors and give them new lives in our society, but some species were all but wiped out." He raised his eyes to look at Xarla. "I am sorry we were not able to save your kind."

She gave him a weak smile. "I don't blame you." Her gaze flicked to the viewscreen. "I lay the blame at the feet of those monsters."

"So, if they're known for wiping out alien species, why would they take us captive?" Hope asked.

Kos set his mouth in a hard line. "They have been attempting to invade Earth for a long time. It is why we defend your planet so faithfully."

Hope cocked her head at him. "That and all the women you kidnap."

"We do not kidnap." His cheeks reddened. "We have a legal treaty with your governments—"

She held up her hands. "Calm down, big guy. I know all that. I'm just taking the piss out of you."

Xarla blinked at him a few times. "How would you remove—?"

"Not actually remove piss," Hope said, shaking her head. "It's an expression. Never mind. What were you saying about the Kronock and why they would take us captive?"

Kos focused on her. "The Kronock have been altering their own biology with technology and also fusing their DNA with other alien DNA to enhance their abilities."

"They're making themselves into super-aliens?" Hope shivered. "Creepy."

"We intercepted intelligence that harvesting human DNA and fusing it with their own is part of their plan to make an invasion of Earth easier," Kos said.

The realization hit Hope, and she put a hand over her mouth. "So, you don't think they'll take all of us captive, you just think they'll take me?"

Kos didn't answer, his gaze shuttering as he spun back around. "I do not know what they will do. I cannot claim to understand the scaly beasts."

"And they have scales?" Hope gaped at Xarla, who gave her a half shrug. "This keeps getting better and better."

Hope took a deep breath and blew it out, trying to remember any of her mother's meditation techniques that she'd dismissed as woo woo nonsense. "So, what are our options? Fly as fast as we can and hope your Drexian buddies reach us in time?"

"We will jump away and hope we can get close enough to Drexian space that we won't be followed."

"Jump?" Hope asked. "Is that like using a transporter beam?"

Kos craned his neck to look at her, one eyebrow raised. "Transporter beam?"

"Never mind. It's a Star Trek thing."

He looked even more confused. "It is a way for us to jump through space. Hard to trace and therefore hard to follow."

"Then let's do that!" Hope said, wondering why they hadn't jumped already, if it was such an easy way to travel.

He faced forward again, his fingers dancing across the console. His shoulders hunched over and he braced his arms. "Preparing to jump. Strap in."

Hope quickly fastened herself into her seat as Xarla did the same. Peering out the front of the shuttle, she saw the gunmetal-gray enemy ship taking shape as it neared them. Even from a distance, the hull looked scaly and menacing.

Come on, let's go, she thought as she tapped her fingers impatiently on the armrest. *I do* not *want to be part of some alien DNA experiment.*

The ship began a countdown in a stilted female voice.

"Three...two...one."

A bright red light flashed, and the ship shuddered, before Hope was pushed back into her seat and the shuttle lurched forward. But instead of seeing the streaks of stars passing like she did when they increased their speed, there was only a flash and then the view outside the ship changed.

There was no more Kronock ship in the distance, and the moon they'd been passing had vanished.

"Did it work?" she asked, although she knew the answer before Kos confirmed it.

"It worked," he said. "The jump was successful."

She let out a relieved sigh. "Are we at the Drexian outpost or wherever we're supposed to be?"

"The shuttle's jump drive does not have enough power to make that kind of jump."

"So, how many more of those until we're back in Drexian space?"

Kos tapped the console, a muscle in the side of his jaw ticking. "We cannot jump again."

Hope noticed that the familiar background hum of the engine was gone, as was the soft vibration she'd grown accustomed to. "Why not?"

Kos swiveled slowly. "We escaped the Kronock, but it seems they got off a shot before we jumped."

CHAPTER
TWENTY-SEVEN

Hope's brow was furrowed as she stared at him. "That's what that red flash was?"

Kos nodded absently as he studied the readouts. If they were correct, the laser fire had caused a fuel leak and the shuttle was hemorrhaging fuel into space. Even from inside, he could smell the scent of char and scorched fuel. They were lucky the laser fire hadn't caused their ship to explode, but if he didn't stop the leak, they would soon be without power.

"At least the Kronock are gone." The relief in Xarla's voice was palpable.

"But where are we?" Hope got out of her chair and moved to sit next to him, leaning so she could see out the front. "There doesn't look like there's anything here."

"That's not a bad thing," he told her, glad for once not to see approaching enemy ships or feel the tug of another ship's tractor beam.

Hope didn't seem so sure as she drummed her fingers on her knees. "But we still aren't close to the Drexian..."

"Outpost," he finished for her. "The space station is still under repairs, so we're heading back to a temporary outpost."

She nodded. "But everything will be the same at this outpost?"

"Not exactly the same," he said. "There is no holographic technology there, so you will not be in a fantasy suite until we return to the station. That is, if you still wish to be in one."

"Why wouldn't I want to be in the fantasy suite? Being on a fake Caribbean island was the coolest part of the whole thing."

"If you do not choose to remain a tribute bride, you do not..."

Her eyebrows popped up. "I forgot. No fancy suites on the low rent side of the station." She crossed her arms over her chest. "Typical."

"Why would you decide against being his bride?" Xarla asked. "I thought you two were...?"

Her words drifted away as Hope shot her a look.

"It doesn't matter," Hope said, not meeting his eyes. "I'll just be glad to get back to solid ground. I've been on one kind of ship or another for ages."

Kos couldn't shake the sinking sensation in the pit of his stomach. It didn't appear that her mind had changed, but he also wasn't sure if he wanted to fight about it anymore.

He turned his attention back to the console, swiping his fingers across the smooth surface. He needed to focus on the mission, which had always been to bring Hope back safely, nothing more and nothing less. The best way to ensure they made it back to Drexian space in one piece was to repair the shuttle and seal the leak. Neither of which he could do sitting in the pilot's chair and feeling sorry for himself.

Standing, he strode to the back of the shuttlecraft. He opened one of the hidden cabinets and retrieved an environmental suit, the shimmering fabric reflecting the ebony interior. He rubbed the sleek material between his fingers. It had been a long time since he'd needed to don one of the high-tech suits, but he remembered them well from his training.

Drexian scientists had developed the fabric, which morphed

colors depending on its surroundings and shrunk to fit the wearer, creating a lightweight outfit that would protect warriors from the elements and even from the harshness of space. Instead of bulky outfits, the Drexian environmental suits had hoods that zipped around the face and provided a steady oxygen flow, while the rest of the suit adhered to the skin and kept the wearer protected from heat, cold, and even radiation.

He shook out the suit and stepped into the legs.

"What are you doing?" Hope asked, joining him in the back, while Xarla remained in the seating area at the front.

He didn't look at her, focusing instead on pulling the black fabric over his hips. "Preparing to fix the ship."

"And you need a flashy jumpsuit to do that?"

"I need an environmental suit so I can go outside the ship safely."

Hope held up both palms. "Wait a second. You can't go out there. It's space."

He glanced at her. "I am aware of that. That is why I am putting on this suit. It will protect me."

Hope touched the fabric covering his leg. "This? It's so thin!"

He pulled the suit up over his waist and slipped his arms in, zipping the front up to his neck. "It was developed to be thin and incredibly strong."

She put a hand to his chest, rubbing her fingers across the iridescent fabric and sending heat ricocheting through him. "I've seen wetsuits that are thicker than this."

He put his hands over hers. "I promise you it's safe."

She pulled her hands out from under his and shook her head. "I don't want you to go out there."

He sighed. He did not have time for this. They were losing more fuel every moment he stayed inside arguing with her. He slapped a band around his wrist that shrunk the suit so that it fit him like a second skin. "I have to."

"No, you don't." Her voice was shrill, although her gaze moved across the form-fitting suit encasing his chest. "You could stay in here with us."

"And what?" he snapped. "Wait until our fuel is gone and then wait until our power goes out and our life support dwindles, and I have to watch you die?"

She drew in a sharp breath. "No, but I don't want…"

His patience unraveled, and he backed her into the wall, pinning her hands to either side of her. "What do you want, Hope? Or do you even have any idea?"

Her eyes were large and dark as she looked up at him. "I know I don't want you to risk your life for me anymore."

"You don't get to decide that." His voice was a near-growl. "You can decide whether you want to be my bride, you can decide to go live in the reject section, you can even decide you don't want to see me again, but you do not get to decide who I risk my life for. You may not be sure about me, but I have always been sure about you. I know that you are mine. You will always be mine. And I will never stop trying to save you."

Her mouth dropped open and a small gasp escaped her lips.

Kos didn't wait for a response. He knew she didn't have one. Crushing his mouth to hers, he pulled her into a tight embrace. Her body went limp, her lips yielding to his as he pressed her harder against the wall. Then her arms were scraping through his hair and pulling him closer. His cock throbbed as she arched into him, the feel of her soft body moving against him sending shockwaves down his spine.

When he finally pulled away, they were both panting.

"If you get to save me, why don't I get to save you?" Hope asked.

He took her face in one hand, stroking his thumb across her bottom lip. Maybe saving her would make up for not being able to save his brother. "You already saved me, *cinnara*. Don't you know that?"

Her breathing was ragged, and her eyes sparkled. "I don't know if I can ever be what you want. I don't know if it's in me."

Her words were like ice in his veins, but he tried to shake them off. "Right now, all I want is for you to be alive and safe. We will worry about the rest later."

Stepping away from her, Kos forced himself to focus his mind on what he needed to do. He flipped up his hood, enclosing his face and tapping his wrist to start the air flow. He grabbed a tool kit from another cabinet, checking it quickly to ensure it had what he needed.

"You're sure I can't talk you out of this?" Hope asked, her words muffled through the hood.

He reached up and twisted the inner ring of the shuttle's top hatch. "Neither of us seem to be skilled at talking the other into anything."

"That's not fair," she said. "You know I..."

He stopped twisting the hatch and waited for her to finish the sentence. He felt like he didn't know anything for sure. Not when it came to the human female who was supposed to be his mate.

"I will be back soon," he said when he realized she wasn't going to speak. He tapped his wrist again. "You can monitor me on the comms system."

She nodded, her eyebrows pressed together as he popped open the inner hatch and hoisted himself up through it. His throat was tight as he took a last look at her before slamming the inner hatch and locking it. He reached up and opened the outer hatch, tethering himself to a hook inside before leaving the shuttle.

The darkness surrounding him was vast, and he swallowed down a sudden flash of panic as it struck him how small their vessel was and how alone they were. Stars blinked in the distance but there were no planets or other ships anywhere in sight.

Forcing himself not to think about how far they were from any other life, Kos turned toward the ship and the steady drops of fuel he saw leaving from the dark hull and floating away. He clenched his jaw and reached for his tools. The only female he'd ever cared about was inside the damaged shuttle, and her survival depended on him.

CHAPTER
TWENTY-EIGHT

Hope watched the hatch above her close, the metal clang echoing through the small interior of the shuttle. She waited below, listening to the sound of the second hatch opening and closing, her gaze never leaving the hole that Kos had disappeared through.

The smell of burnt oil was stronger in the back of the shuttle, and she had to put a hand over her nose to keep from choking, the taste of char creeping down her throat anyway.

"Why don't you come back and sit down?" Xarla put an arm around her shoulders, her tail wrapping around Hope's waist as she led her back to the chairs in the cockpit.

Hope numbly sat. "I shouldn't have let him go."

"You heard what he said. It was either that or we lose all power in the ship. He's a big, tough Drexian. He'll be fine."

Hope met the alien's large green eyes. "I shouldn't have let him go out there thinking I don't care about him."

Xarla gave her a knowing smile. "I don't think he believes that. You did give him a pretty enthusiastic send-off from what I could hear up here."

Hope's face warmed. "But why can't I tell him?"

"Tell him what?" Xarla tilted her head as she stroked the end of her own tail.

"Oh, I don't know. What I really feel, I guess." Hope peered out the front of the ship, but she saw nothing. No surprise there. If Kos was repairing a fuel leak, he was probably at the back of the vessel. She flopped back.

"And what do you really feel?"

There was that question again. Why was it so hard to answer? Why was it so difficult to say the words?

Xarla studied her for a while. "I don't need for you to tell me. It's obvious to anyone watching the two of you that you're in love."

"What?" Hope snapped her head around to look at the alien. "In love? Who said anything about that? I barely know the guy."

Xarla twitched one shoulder up and down. "As if that matters. I fell in love with my Kerx about two ternons after I laid eyes on him."

"Ternons?"

"Vralithian unit of measuring time." She snapped her fingers. "As long as that."

"So, two seconds," Hope said. "You fell in love with a guy in two seconds?"

Xarla leaned back, a smile spreading across her face. "Almost as soon as I saw him." She sighed. "He had a very long, very fine tail."

Hope couldn't help grinning herself, wondering if a long tail meant anything else in Xarla's species. "His name was Kerx?"

Her friend nodded. "He was the most amazing male I'd ever met. We were bonded almost immediately."

"Is that like being married?"

Xarla cocked her head in obvious confusion.

Hope tried again. "Mated?"

Xarla bobbed her head up and down. "Yes, we were mates for life."

Hope swallowed a lump she didn't know had been growing in her throat. "And then you were taken by the Curator?"

"Oh, no. Kerx was killed in the second wave of the Kronock invasion. I wasn't taken by the Curator until much later, although by that time I barely cared. With Kerx gone, nothing mattered anymore."

"I'm really sorry," Hope said.

Xarla waved a hand, seeming to snap out of her memory. "It was a long time ago, but I can tell you from experience that time doesn't matter when it comes to falling in love."

"You were lucky to know right away. It's not like that with me. I don't have those same kinds of feelings."

"You don't?" Xarla squinted at her. "Do humans not fall in love?"

"We do, it's just that love has never been high up on my to-do list."

Xarla let out a peal of laughter. "It isn't something you plan for. It just happens to you. And unless I'm very wrong, it's already happened to you and Kos."

At the mention of his name, Hope glanced outside again, even though she knew she wouldn't see him. She hoped everything was going well and wished she'd thought to ask him how long the repair would take. Waiting had never been one of her strengths.

"Obviously, I care about him," she said, when she'd turned her attention back to Xarla. "How could I not after all we've been through together? And it's not like he isn't a really great guy. If we were back on Earth, I'd definitely want to hook up with him again."

Her alien friend looked bewildered again. "Hook up? That sounds painful."

"It means get together."

Another blank look from Xarla.

"Sleep with? Have sex with? Fuck?"

Xarla smiled and nodded. "Ah, yes. Like you did in your cell?"

Hope tried not to act flustered. "You knew about that?"

Xarla swiveled her chair around. "You were not as quiet as you thought you were. But don't worry, you weren't as loud as the

Bragadinlings who occupied the cell before you. All those tentacles and suckers made quite a racket."

"I guess that's something," Hope muttered to herself, glad that Kos didn't have tentacles. "Anyway, the sex was great, but it doesn't mean we're stuck with each other for life."

"Humans don't mate for life?"

"Not this human."

Xarla tapped one yellow finger to her chin. "And you have told this to Kos? That you don't intend to take just one Drexian?"

"I don't want to mate with more than one Drexian."

"Then I do not understand."

Hope was starting not to understand herself, either. "It isn't that I want another Drexian, it's that I can't imagine saying yes to one guy for life."

Xarla nodded slowly, but Hope was pretty sure she didn't get it, and her head was starting to hurt from explaining and getting nowhere, especially when her reasons sounded so lame, even to her.

"Shouldn't we have heard from Kos by now?" she asked, glancing at the console and the confusing display of lights and symbols. At least the scent of scorched fuel had dissipated. That had to be a good sign.

"He mentioned the comms system." Xarla studied the shiny surface. "Maybe we have to press something to talk to him."

Hope inspected the readouts. No way was she going to press an unknown button and potentially activate a missile or something. "I don't think we should mess with the controls."

"Here." Xarla ignored her, reaching across and touching a finger to a green button. "Let's see if that worked."

Hope waited but heard nothing but static.

"Say something," whispered Xarla.

"Kos?" She raised her voice, even though she suspected the comms system could pick up her voice easily. "Are you out there?"

There was a heavy pause, then his deep voice. "I'm here."

She let out a breath as Xarla clapped her hands. "How's it going?"

"I've been able to stop the leak." His voice sounded distant, even though he was only on the other side of the ship's wall. "Now I'm patching the rip in the hull. Is everything okay inside?"

"We're fine." She wanted to tell him she missed him, but that sounded pathetic. He'd been gone for only a few minutes.

"Good. I should have this done shortly, and we can resume our flight."

"Be careful out there," she said, ignoring Xarla's amused grin.

"I will...*Grek!*"

"Kos." Hope sat up abruptly. "Is everything all right?"

"I dropped one of my tools. The one I need to seal this hole." He huffed out a loud breath. "I've almost got it."

Even though she knew she couldn't do anything from inside, Hope jumped up and craned her neck to try to see him out the front.

"*Grek!*"

His shout made her breath catch in her throat. "What's going on out there? Kos?"

Xarla joined her in standing, but all they could hear was static.

Hope locked eyes with the alien next to her. "Where did he go?"

"I'm still here." Kos's voice broke through the static. "But I don't know for how long."

"What do you mean?" Hope asked.

"When I went for the sealing tool, my tether unhooked from the ship."

Hope sank back down in her chair, her legs shaky. "I don't understand. What does that mean?"

"I'm no longer attached to the ship."

Xarla reached out and clutched her arm, and Hope followed her gaze. Since the suit had adjusted itself to match the inky blackness of the sky, it was almost impossible to see, but Kos's face was clear as he floated by in space.

Hope stood again, her mouth going dry as she met his eyes across the distance. "Can't you get back to us?"

His chuckle was a little sad. "There is no air in space, so I can't propel myself through it nor can I stop moving away."

Xarla inhaled sharply and sank down into her seat, pulling her tail into her lap.

"Then I'm coming to get you." Hope headed to the back of the shuttle and started opening the hidden cabinets until she found one of the environmental suits.

"Absolutely not," Kos's voice boomed through the ship.

"Do I have to remind you for the hundredth time, you're not the boss of me?" She stepped into the baggy suit—clearly designed for bigger Drexians—tugging it over her waist and ignoring Kos yelling at her to stop.

Her heart was racing and all the sounds around her had become a single loud blur. She could not let him die out in space. She couldn't. The thought of losing him made her almost double over in pain as she jammed her arms into the suit and zipped it up.

Maybe Xarla was right. Maybe she did love him, but if this was love, it felt like shit. At least, the thought of being without him felt awful, as if a gaping hole was being opened in her heart.

This was why you never got attached, she reminded herself. Well, it was too fucking late for that. She was attached, and even though she wasn't sure what it all meant or how it would play out, him dying, when she could save him, was not an option.

Shaking her head, she stared up at the hatch. She didn't know how she was going to get him back, but she was going to do it. The alternative was unthinkable, and she pushed the thoughts of him floating alone in space from her mind. She didn't know how much air he had in that suit, but it couldn't be a lot.

No, no, no. That was not going to happen. She was going to get him back. He was not going to die all alone thinking she didn't love him. Even thinking the word almost made her burst into tears. She loved him. Of course, she loved him. Why else would she be crawling out of a spaceship to save him? It was possibly the stupidest thing she'd ever done, and that was saying something.

She sized up the distance to the hatch. She wasn't as tall as Kos, but she should be able to make it if she jumped high. Crouching down, she felt a sharp pain on the back of her head. What the hell? She put her hand to her head as she swayed in place, the ship seeming to tilt suddenly.

As her vision blurred and she collapsed to the floor, she heard Xarla's voice. "I'm so sorry."

CHAPTER

TWENTY-NINE

"Thanks, Xarla," Kos said, once the alien had come on the comms system to tell him she'd knocked out Hope. "You're sure she's just knocked out?"

He could see the outline of the Vralithian through the front window of the shuttle but was too far away to see detail or he knew he'd see the female's stern expression.

"I'm sure. She's breathing fine, but she might have a headache when she wakes up." Xarla sighed heavily. "I'm not happy about this. She's never going to forgive me."

"You saved her life," he said, letting out a breath of relief that Hope wouldn't be able to follow him out into space to her own almost certain death. "I owe you one."

"I don't know if you're going to be able to pay up, Drexian." Xarla's voice cracked.

Kos tried to laugh, but it came out choked. "Then you'll just have to accept my eternal gratitude."

The dark hull of the shuttle was so close, but without gravity or any form of propulsion, he couldn't get himself to it. At least he felt close to her, he thought, as he worked to suppress the growing sense of panic that he was floating in space with no external source of oxygen.

Swiveling his head, Kos couldn't spot anything aside from vast open space. He knew there were no planets nearby, and as far as he could see, no other ships. He'd sent out a quick subspace distress call, but he'd encrypted it and put in on a Drexian-only channel. Luck would have to be on his side for a Drexian ship to be close enough to get it in time. And, so far, he hadn't been all that lucky.

Except for Hope. He'd been lucky to find Hope. She might have been a pain in his ass at first, but he wouldn't give up any of it for the time they'd had together. Not even if it led him to where he was now.

"I can try to fly the shuttle over to you," Xarla said, her pale gold face appearing larger through the front of the ship as she sat in the pilot's chair. "You aren't far away."

"Have you ever piloted a ship before?"

A long pause. "Technically, no."

What little hope he'd had slipped farther away. "Chances are greater you'd fly into me than be able to accelerate just enough to reach me."

"I have to try," Xarla said, her voice becoming a whisper. "I couldn't look your female in the eye if I didn't."

"I appreciate you wanting to—"

"Listen, Drexian." She cut him off. "Drop the tough guy act. I know you don't want to die out there, and there's no way I'm going to let you without at least trying to save you. I know your female enough to know she'll never get over losing you. I'm not going to be responsible for that, and neither are you, so you can either tell me how to fly this thing or hope for the best."

He almost laughed at the bossy tone of the alien. "Then I'd better walk you through it."

"Now we're talking. Okay, what do I do first?"

Kos closed his eyes, envisioning the shiny black control panel as if he was sitting in the pilot's chair. He imagined placing his hands on the smooth surface that was always slightly cool to the touch. "Since I stopped the fuel leak, you should be able to power up the engines again."

"How do I do that?"

He kept his eyes closed. Imagining himself piloting the shuttle helped calm his pounding heart, and if he thought hard enough he could almost smell the slight aroma of burned fuel and hear the low hum of the engines powering up. "Find the green symbol that looks like a sideways oval with a line through the center. It's to your far right."

Xarla hummed softly. "Found it."

"Press that and hold it until you hear the engine catch." Even through the static of the comms link, Kos could hear the subtle purr of the shuttle powering up.

"Did it!" Xarla's voice was filled with pride. "Now what?"

"Now the hard part." He opened his eyes, breathing in and feeling the air in his mask becoming thin. "You'll need to navigate using only thrusters."

"Thrusters," Xarla repeated. "Where are those?"

He pulled up the flashing lights of the console in his mind again. Even though, before he'd come on this mission, it had been a long time since he'd flown small vessels, his Drexian Academy training had kicked in as soon as he'd sat down in the pilot's chair. Now, he used muscle memory as well as visual recall to remember the controls.

"To your left. Two vertical panels side by side. The one to the left powers the left thruster—"

"And the one to the right powers the right thruster," Xarla finished for him, clearly eager. "Got it."

"Moving that small a distance is going to require a soft touch. Too fast and you'll overshoot me by a lot." He didn't say what he was thinking. If she went too far, she might not be able to find him again.

Her long exhalation told him she was more nervous that she wanted to let on. "Gentle and slow. No problem."

Kos sized up the distance and his position with regard to the shuttle. "Engage the left thruster just a bit."

Xarla's wide green eyes met his through the front glass of the shuttle. "Ready?"

He nodded, his throat too dry for him to respond. If this didn't work...

She looked back down at the console, and then the shuttle moved forward slightly.

She'd taken his advice to heart. He'd never seen a spaceship move so slowly. At least she wasn't in danger of overshooting him, although at this rate he might run out of oxygen before she reached him.

Her head popped up. "Did it work?"

"That was good," he said. "Just a few more like that and you've got it."

He saw her head whip around and heard her let out one of the Earth curses that Hope was so fond of.

"She's waking up."

"That's okay," he said, spots dancing in front of his eyes from the thinning oxygen. "Focus on the thruster."

"Right." She turned back around. "Thruster."

The shuttle lurched forward, this time a bit farther, although it was directly in front of him. One more acceleration, and he'd be splayed across the front glass of the ship.

Kos sucked in a breath, but it hitched in his throat. No more air. "You need to adjust to your right," he gasped. "Hurry."

Xarla looked up, her mouth falling open as she locked on to him, and then her gaze traveled beyond him. He could see Hope behind her as she made her way to the front of the cockpit, and then both women gaping past him. His head throbbed as his brain ran out of oxygen, but he was not scared to die. Not when he saw Hope.

She would survive. He had saved her. For the first time since he'd seen his brother vanish before his eyes, Kos felt like he had succeeded. Pride and love filled his chest and warmed him, as he tried to focus on her face through the ship's glass. She was looking past him, though. At what?

Even as his vision blurred and his ears rang, Kos managed to turn his head slowly until he could see the enormous dark-hulled ship hovering behind him.

Hope's voice screaming his name was the last thing he heard as he felt his body spasm.

CHAPTER

THIRTY

"Kos!" Hope's head throbbed as she held herself steady behind the pilot's seat where Xarla sat. She wasn't sure if she was seeing things or if the Drexian was really floating between them and a massive black ship.

His body twisted to face the ship, and then he appeared to go limp.

"Oh no," Xarla whispered. "I think he ran out of air."

"What?" Hope sank into the nearest seat, her legs too unsteady to support her as she gaped at the alien vessel that dwarfed them. "How long have I been out? Wait a second, what happened to me? Did you knock me out?"

Xarla didn't look back at her. "Only because Kos begged me to. You going out there with him was a suicide mission."

Hope tried to look away from the sight of Kos's form seemingly suspended in space, but she couldn't. "But now he's..."

Xarla turned her attention to the console. "Maybe I can still maneuver the ship to get him. I just need to use the thrusters to get close enough."

Hope stared at Xarla as her fingers tapped the console. "Seriously, how long have I been unconscious? When did you learn to fly this thing?"

"Kos gave me a crash course," Xarla said, edging the shuttle forward slightly.

Kos's body jerked back, and Hope gasped as he was pulled toward the other ship. "Who is that? Is it the Kronock?" She jumped up, ignoring the dizziness. "We have to stop them."

"I can't stop them," Xarla said, her hands frozen as they hovered above the controls. "They have some sort of tractor beam on him."

"Maybe we can shoot at them," Hope suggested. "This thing does have some weapons, right? Let's fire at them!"

"What if we hit Kos?" Xarla waved a hand at the Drexian being drawn through space by some sort of invisible beam. "I've never fired a torpedo or laser."

"I'll do it," Hope said, her gaze desperately raking across the unfamiliar lights and symbols of the console. "I have to do something. I can't lose him again."

Xarla grabbed her by the shoulders. "Him being taken captive is better than us accidentally blasting him out of the sky."

Hope shook her head, panic fluttering in her belly. "Not if it's the Kronock. Not if they torture him." She tried to pull herself from Xarla surprisingly strong grip. "We can't let that happen."

The alien shook her hard enough to make Hope stop struggling. "We're outmatched when it comes to weapons, so I don't think firing anything will help, but I also don't think that's a Kronock ship."

Hope steadied her jagged breathing, narrowing her eyes past Xarla and watching Kos being pulled into a hatch on the sleek ship. "You don't?"

"I'm not an expert, but the Kronock ships I remember looked much scarier."

Hope thought back to the ship they'd run from. "And scalier."

"Not to mention," Xarla said, "if this was a Kronock ship, they wouldn't be rescuing a Drexian, and they would already be boarding us."

Hope's pulse evened out. "Then let's really hope you're right. Can we hail them and find out?"

Xarla scrunched her mouth as she studied the console, finally pressing a button. "Here goes nothing."

"Alien vessel," Hope said when she heard the faint sound of static indicating that there was an open line. She tried to make her voice sound official, channeling every sci-fi show she'd ever seen back when she was on Earth. Maybe if she was convincing enough, the ship would give him back. "This is a Drexian vessel, and you are committing an act of war by abducting our warrior."

Xarla turned and raised her eyebrows at Hope, nodding her encouragement.

Hope took a deep breath when she got no response. "Release our crew man at once."

"Drexian vessel," a deep voice responded. "This is also a Drexian vessel."

"What?" Hope abandoned her serious tone. "You're Drexians?"

"This is Captain Varden. To whom am I speaking?"

"Hope." She collapsed into a chair. "My name is Hope."

"And I'm Xarla." The Vralithian waved toward the other ship.

"Hope? The tribute bride Kos went searching for?" the captain of the Drexian ship asked, his voice registering surprise.

Hope couldn't answer. She knew if she tried to speak, she'd start bawling. The ship wasn't an enemy ship that was going to kill them or take them for bizarre experiments. They'd been found by the Drexians. They'd been rescued just in time. After everything that had happened, they were going to be all right. Hope closed her eyes and squeezed them tight to keep the tears from falling.

"That's the one," Xarla said, when she saw that Hope wasn't responding. "Speaking of Kos, is he okay?"

Varden paused and there were voices behind him. "He's fine.

We've taken him to our medical bay for a full work-up, but he's breathing again."

Hope put her face in her hands and leaned forward, bracing her elbows on her knees. Now that she knew he was going to be fine, her body began to tremble.

"That's wonderful news," Xarla said, spinning around to face her. "Isn't that wonderful news?"

Hope tried to reply, but she was too busy wiping away the tears that were streaming down her face. Xarla's luminous green eyes widened, then filled with tears as well. The alien threw her arms around her, and the two women burst into tears.

"Hope?" A high-pitched voice came over the comms system. "Is that really you? Oh, dear. It sounds like they're wailing." More muffled voices in the background. "You're sure she's all right?"

Hope jerked her head up. She recognized that voice. "Reina?"

Reina let out a loud sigh. "It's me. I'm so happy to hear your voice, dear. We've been looking all over for you and Kos. I've been worried sick."

"What? How?" Hope's cries were replaced by laughs of disbelief. "How did you get on a Drexian ship? The last I heard you'd been sold off by those wanker pirates."

Reina tittered. "Those pirates weren't very nice, were they? I think they were 'wankers,' as you put it. Luckily, they sold me to a trader who was more than happy to return me to the Drexians. Apparently, he owed the Drexians anyway. I was returned to the temporary outpost rather quickly."

Hope hadn't known how much she'd missed the nervous Vexling until she heard her voice. "Then how did you end up on a Drexian ship looking for us?"

"I insisted on coming, of course," Reina said. "I thought you'd like to see a familiar face after your ordeal. I can be very persuasive when I need to be, hon. Don't forget, I work with human brides for a living."

Hope laughed. "How could I forget?" Reina had passed the time when they were being held captive by relaying her wildest wedding stories. "I'm really glad you came, and I'm even more relieved you were returned to the Drexians. What about the other women and Serge?"

"No word on the Inferno Force mission," Reina said, her voice breaking slightly, "but I have no doubt they'll find the other tributes and Serge."

"I'm sure you're right."

"But for now, our mission is to get you and your mate back to the Drexian outpost," Reina said. "Are you ready to go home?"

Hope hesitated. She wasn't sure if she was ready to call the Drexian outpost home, but as long as Kos would be there, she was happy.

"More than ready."

CHAPTER
THIRTY-ONE

Kos noticed the smell first. Sharp and astringent and nothing like the scent of leaking fuel. He opened his eyes, immediately flinching from the bright overhead lights.

Well, he wasn't floating in space anymore, but he also wasn't in the shuttle. Soft whirring noises were accompanied by intermittent beeping. Nope, definitely not space.

The last thing he remembered was floating near the shuttle and trying to guide Xarla as she steered the shuttle to intercept him. He'd been so close and then... What?

He could recall sucking in a breath and feeling the sharp tug as he drew in no air. Then he'd turned and seen... a ship. The memory came into focus. A Drexian ship.

Kos raised a sluggish hand to shield his eyes as he opened them again. Was he really on a Drexian ship? He let his eyes adjust to the light until he could peer around him without the glare making his head ache. What he saw made him let out a loud sigh of relief.

He was in a compact three-bed sick bay with shiny metal countertops and mechanical metal arms tucked up into the ceiling. A machine on a nearby stand was humming and flashing readouts of what he assumed were his vitals. Glancing down, he could see that he was naked except for a crisp white sheet that was tucked around his hips, and the bed he lay in was slightly inclined.

The door slid open, and Captain Varden strode into the room. "They told me you were waking."

Kos attempted to sit up, but Varden shook his head. "Don't move. You need to save your strength. They're bringing your bride over now."

Kos raised an eyebrow in question.

"She seems quite eager to see you and also quite upset that you think you can keep trying to tell her what she can and can't do." Varden crossed his arms and rocked back on his heels. "That's a direct quote."

"I'll bet it is," Kos said, although his chest swelled at the thought of seeing Hope again. He didn't even care if she was angry. Actually, he rather enjoyed how her eyes blazed and her cheeks flushed when she was busy arguing with him.

Varden ran a hand through his salt-and-pepper hair. "You want to tell me what happened out there after you left Captain Brok? I didn't mind sacrificing my first officer to rescue his tribute bride, but I take some issue with you becoming part of the Curator's collection."

Kos readjusted himself on the bed, wishing he was more formally attired for the debrief with his commanding officer. "I ran into some unexpected issues with the tribute, and while we were sorting things out, our ship was boarded."

Varden nodded, his brow furrowed. "So, this Curator is real?"

"Unfortunately. So are all the stories. Actually, the stories don't do him justice. Sir, he's running a floating zoo and holding all sorts of creatures captive."

Varden's frown deepened into a scowl. "How has he evaded capture for all this time?"

"From what I could tell, he has important friends and clients. Some of the guests at his party looked like they moved in elevated circles."

"Anyone we can use to flush him out?" Varden asked.

"Possibly." Kos squared his shoulders. "Captain, I'd like to be a part of the mission to find this criminal."

"I thought you might. Does that mean you're requesting another leave of absence from the station?"

"The station is not back to full operation yet, is it?" Kos asked. "Otherwise, you probably wouldn't have been able to take a ship to come after me."

"You are correct that they are still rebuilding after the attack, but I don't know that I wouldn't have come after you regardless," Varden told him. "You are my first officer and were with me when we crashed on the primitive planet after the evacuation. After all we've been through together, I couldn't exactly let someone else go after you."

Kos looked down at his lap, his throat unexpectedly thick with emotion. "Thank you, sir."

"You are an exemplary officer, Kos. You always have been." Varden took a deep breath. "But I've always felt your talents might be wasted on my bridge."

Kos's head snapped up. "Sir?"

"Don't get me wrong. I don't want to lose you. It will be impossible to find an officer who can fill your shoes, but I also know that it might be time for you to take on new challenges." Varden grinned. "And not just the challenge of your tribute bride, although I suspect you might have your hands full there, as well."

Kos's cheeks warmed. He didn't know what to say, although if he was being honest, he knew his commanding officer was right. "I would never abandon my commitments, Captain."

"I know you wouldn't. Your loyalty does you credit. That is why I'm recommending you for your own command."

Kos's mouth fell open. "My own command?"

"I am not the only one who believes you deserve this. Captain Brok sent me a subspace message that amounted to the same thing.

He was quite impressed by you." Varden tilted his head. "Thinks you should consider Inferno Force."

Kos managed to close his mouth. "I don't know what to say, sir."

Varden shook his head. "You don't have to make any final decisions at the moment. And I suspect you'll want to run your options by your mate."

Kos dropped his eyes. "I do not think she is my mate, sir."

"Really?" The captain cocked an eyebrow. "That's not the impression I got."

"Things are more complicated than I anticipated they would be."

Varden threw his head back and laughed. "Things are always more complicated when it comes to human females. Do you remember what happened with me and my mate?"

Kos did remember. He'd had a front row seat to the captain's bumbling missteps before things finally worked out.

"Take it from me," Captain Varden said. "It does not have to be so complicated. As long as you care for her, you can work it out."

"I'm not so sure," Kos said, feeling the old ache return. "She has made it clear she has no intention of being anyone's mate."

Varden shrugged. "That is what Dakar's mate said, as well. Human females are known for changing their minds." He held up a finger. "But it is very important you never remind them that they changed their mind. They do not like that at all."

Kos couldn't help grinning. "How is your bride, Captain?"

Varden's cheeks flushed. "Very well. She is expecting our first child."

Kos could feel the Drexian's joy and pride as if they were oozing from his pores. "Congratulations, sir."

Varden cleared his throat and nodded, his eyes shining. Before either man could break the silence, the door glided open, and Hope stomped into the room.

"You have a lot of explaining to do, Drexian," she said, folding her arms over her chest and glaring at him.

Captain Varden backed away, shooting him a final sympathetic glance as he slipped out of the room.

Hope still wore the long, flowing dress she'd been given on the Curator's ship, but it looked considerably worse for wear, with tears and smudges he hadn't noticed before. Her blonde hair was pulled up into a messy bun, and her flushed cheeks were streaked with tears. His heart constricted at the sight of her.

Even though she looked furious, he didn't care. He'd never been as happy to see anyone before in his life. Before he could tell her that, her chin started to quiver.

She ran to him and jumped onto his bed, covering his body with hers and kissing him hard. When she pulled away, he took a startled breath. "I thought you wanted me to explain."

Hope kissed him again, nipping at his bottom lip. "First things first, big guy."

CHAPTER

THIRTY-TWO

"I don't understand," Kos said, his hands firmly on her hips as she straddled him. "I thought you were angry at me."

"Oh, I am." Hope took his face in both of her hands. "I'm furious. I can't believe you actually told Xarla to incapacitate me so I couldn't leave the ship. She's apologized, by the way."

"You wish for me to apologize for keeping you from killing yourself?"

"I wasn't trying to kill myself. I was trying to save your ass."

His eyes narrowed at her. "Your saving my ass could have killed you."

Hope leaned back and tried to ignore the very hard, very large bulge underneath her. "You would have done it for me."

"That's because I..."

She angled her head at him. "That's because what? You're a guy? You're a Drexian warrior?"

"No." He lifted a hand to brush aside a tendril of hair that had fallen down on her forehead. "Because I love you."

Hope felt like all the air had been knocked out of her. No man had ever told her that, aside from the ones who were trying to get in her pants, and those didn't count. She locked eyes with him and swallowed hard, knowing in that moment that she felt the same way about him and, as much as she'd tried to fight it, she knew she had for a while "Well, I love you too."

He held her gaze, his gray eyes searching hers. "You do?"

She nodded, feeling tears prick the backs of her eyes. She'd gone from being a girl who never cried to one who couldn't seem to stop the waterworks. "I mean, I know it's ridiculous, because we hardly know each other, but I guess we've already been through a lot, and—"

Kos pulled her down into a kiss before she could finish her sentence. She allowed herself to sink into the softness of his lips before tearing her mouth from his. "Are you trying to shut me up by kissing me?"

"Of course not, but you do not need to explain it to me, mate." The corner of his mouth quirked up. "If I was trying to shut you up, I would do this."

He swatted her ass sharply, and Hope yelped.

She rubbed a hand on her backside. "I can't believe you fucking spanked me. I thought the only reason you did that on the Curator's ship was to help us escape."

"It was." Kos palmed one ass cheek and squeezed. "But I discovered that I liked it more than I thought I would."

He pulled her down again and captured her mouth, parting her lips and stroking her tongue as he gave her ass another hard slap. Even though she tried to wiggle away, Kos held her in place, one hand tangled in her hair and the other firmly gripping her ass.

His kisses were intoxicating, and a pulse of heat throbbed between her legs. She didn't want to admit how much him spanking her turned her on, or how she could already feel that her thighs were slick with arousal. Hope ground herself into the hard bar of his cock, feeling a rush of pleasure as he moaned in her mouth.

He gave her another spank, and she rocked her hips into him, the mix of pleasure and pain sending scorching heat through her.

Kos slid his hands underneath the bunched-up fabric of her dress, sliding his fingers so that they teased her slick opening.

"So wet for me." His voice was husky when he pulled his mouth away from her. "I think you like me spanking you, too."

"You wish." Her words came out between pants, but she tipped her head back and moaned when he slapped her ass cheek.

"I do wish. I wish for you to ride my cock."

She looked over her shoulder furtively. "What if someone comes in?"

Kos pushed one thick finger inside her, and she bit her bottom lip to keep from letting out another loud groan.

"They will probably walk out just as quickly," he said, his gaze locked on her face as he pressed deeper inside her. He was right about that. Anyone who happened to walk into the medical bay would get a lot more than they'd bargained for. At the moment, though, she didn't care. Kos was alive, and they were finally together without any scary aliens after them. She didn't know what the future held, but at the moment all she cared about was how she felt right then, with him.

Hope braced one hand on his bare chest, her eyelids fluttering as he moved his finger inside her. When he slid a second finger inside, she dug her fingernails into his flesh.

"More, "she whispered.

Kos shifted his hand until one of his fingers found her clit, and he slowly circled it as he pumped his fingers into her. The sensations made her body jerk, but Kos held her in place, pulling her mouth to his. Her cries were swallowed by his urgent kisses, his tongue matching the caresses of his fingers.

Hope tilted her ass up, her legs open wide as she straddled him. With each deep stroke of his fingers, he deftly swirled her swollen nub until she was writhing, and her legs were trembling.

When pleasure began to ripple through her, she tore her mouth from his and arched her back, her heat clenching tight around his fingers. "Kos," she gasped, her body bucking.

"Do you want my cock inside you?" he asked, pulling his fingers out and lifting her hips. He pulled down the sheet, his rigid cock springing up.

Her gaze fell to it, and she wet her lips. "Oh, yeah."

Hope took the base in one hand as she raised herself up so that his crown was notched at her opening. She dragged it through her wetness and savored the sound of his needy moan. She met his molten gaze. "You want me to ride you?"

A rough grunt was his only reply as he grasped her by the hips and drove her down on him. Hope heard her own breathy cry as she took him all the way, her body stretching to handle his girth.

"You fill me so good," she said, her eyes rolling back in her head as he lifted her and brought her down again. Like the sharp spanks that made her ass sting, she loved the initial pain that quickly morphed into intense pleasure when she took his huge cock.

As he slid her up and down his shaft in a steady rhythm, Hope cupped her own breasts, thumbing the hard points of her nipples through the sheer fabric.

Kos's pupils flared as he watched her. "Gods, Hope."

"You like that?" she asked, smiling down at him and feeling her release building again.

"You drive me crazy." His fingers bit into her flesh, and he clenched his jaw as he slammed her down on his cock.

Hope pinched her own nipples hard, the sharp sensation making her body detonate. She came even harder than the first time, her body spasming around him.

Kos arched his back as he drove her down and held himself deep, roaring his release, his heat pulsing into her.

Dropping her hands to his chest, which was damp with sweat, Hope sagged against him. "You drive me crazy, too, but I love it." She hitched in a breath. "I love you."

He wrapped his shaky arms around her and held her tight. His heart raced, the thumping practically echoing in her own body. "I love you, too, *cinnara*. Always."

The door slid open, and there was a high-pitched yelp.

"Oh, pardon me. I was looking for the bride," Reina said. "Good heavens. I guess I found her. I suppose now isn't the best time to talk about the bonding ceremony. No, clearly not, although it looks like we're going to need one. Maybe I'll just go talk to the... Oh, my. Maybe I'll just go."

There was a rustling at the door as Reina stumbled back, and the door slid closed again.

"See?" Kos's laughter made her chest shake. "Now you have to be my mate."

"If I have to," Hope said, with a pretend sigh of impatience.

Kos slapped her ass. "It looks like someone needs another spanking."

Hope kissed him hard. "Yes, please."

CHAPTER
THIRTY-THREE

"I wish we were doing this on the Boat," Reina said, wringing her hands as she fluffed the sheer net veil behind Hope. "You could have had your pick of stunning ceremony locations. My personal favorite is the Cape Cod seaside bluff, but Serge favors the butterfly garden."

"It's fine." Hope looked at the reflection of the willowy alien in the mirror behind her. "I don't need a butterfly garden to marry Kos."

Reina's blue swirl of hair popped up over Hope's shoulder. "I know, I know, but this barebones outpost is a far cry from the holographic environments I'm used to using for weddings."

Hope smoothed the front of her ivory gown, the silk soft under her fingers. Even though there were no holodecks, she was thrilled that they'd made it back to the temporary Drexian outpost without any more issues. And since they were in the large ship piloted by Captain Varden, they'd made the trip in a few jumps instead of several days of space flight.

"I don't mind," Hope told Reina, for what felt like the hundredth time since they'd returned. "I'm not used to fancy digs anyway. I was a travel blogger, remember? Cheap hotels and hostels were more my style back on Earth, so even this room is an upgrade."

She glanced around the spacious studio with the large bed to one side and a sunken sitting area featuring beige furniture. The remains of the breakfast she'd been too nervous to eat sat on the low, round coffee table, and a clear ice bucket stood to one side, the bottle of bubbly bobbing in the melted ice. She hadn't had time to personalize the space, but it was still one of the nicest places she'd ever lived. The fact that Kos shared it with her was icing on the cake.

"I still don't know what a blogger is, but I'm glad you're happy with your suite." Reina moved around in front of her as she continued to fluff the veil. "Let's just hope the repairs on the station go well and you'll be back in your fantasy suite soon."

"It still seems strange that we'll actually live in a holographic suite even after we're married."

"Unless Kos takes up a post off the station and you go with him. Not all our matched couples stay on the Boat forever."

Hope nodded, plucking her glass flute of Drexian bubbly off the side table and taking a swig. It wasn't cold anymore, but the bubbles were sweet, and it made her stomach less jumpy. It still made her nervous to think about forever, but her jitters were subsiding as time passed. What would have sent her into a full-fledged panic a week ago now just gave her a mild case of butterflies.

Kos had been talking about not returning to the Boat and his job as first officer. She knew he really wanted to lead the hunting party that went after the Curator, and she didn't blame him. She would love to be there when they found the creepy alien and strung him up for his crimes.

She also knew that Kos had been toying with the idea of joining Inferno Force. She didn't know much about the elite group, but she knew that they were known as the biggest badasses in the Drexian empire, and that was saying something. Hope wasn't sure if Inferno

Force normally allowed their warriors to bring mates with them, but if they didn't, they'd have to relax their rules for her. After everything that had happened, she wasn't letting Kos out of her sight.

"Hope?" Reina's voice jolted her out of her thoughts.

"I'm sorry, what?"

Reina laughed. "I was just saying that we're lucky that Monti and Randi were able to whip up your dress even though they weren't able to get all their supplies off the Boat."

"It's pretty simple." Hope eyed the column of silk that scooped low in the front and hugged her hips to flare out in a slight train at the back.

"I suppose we're lucky Serge isn't here. He would have been horrified that there is no lace and not a single bead." She sucked in a shaky breath. "He's going to be so upset he missed this."

Hope turned and patted Reina's hand. "He would be really proud of you. You've been an amazing wedding planner."

Reina fluttered a hand in front of her face. "Oh, I'm not a wedding planner. Not yet. I'm still a bride liaison."

"You were my wedding planner," Hope insisted. "And I couldn't have asked for a better one. You've pulled everything together with no time and none of the usual bells and whistles you have on the Boat. You are a miracle worker."

Reina's gray cheeks became a patchwork of pink and red. "Aren't you sweet? It's been my honor." She dabbed at her eyes. "And, to be honest, it's kept me busy, so I don't have to worry about Serge and the other tributes."

"Inferno Force will find them," Hope said. "If anyone can, it's those guys."

Reina nodded, and her hair bobbled on her head. "You're right. Of course, you're right. It's just not the same without him."

A beep at the door made them both turn, and a tiny woman swept into the room holding a large box, her tower of pink curls protruding above it.

"Cerise!" Reina bustled forward, taking the white box from the woman. "Is this the bouquet?"

The alien who had been assisting Reina with the wedding planning beamed at both of them. "Preston packed it in lots of tissue paper. He said it was crucial not to touch the flowers when you pick it up."

Reina placed the box gingerly on the coffee table and lifted the lid. Even from a few feet away, Hope could smell the sweet scent of the flowers filling the room.

Reina inhaled deeply. "What did you say these were again?"

"Gardenias." Hope walked over and looked down at the white flowers. "They're my mother's favorite flower."

Even though she'd never been close to her mother—and the woman probably had no idea she'd been taken from Earth—she still felt comforted by having a reminder of her in her wedding. Somehow, loving Kos and knowing how much he loved her—and that he would never leave her—had made it easier to forgive her mother. And easier to move on.

"It's almost time," Cerise said. "Kos is already in place."

Hope tossed back the rest of the alien champagne, the bubbles tickling her nose. "Then let's do this."

Reina fluttered around her, working her hands nervously. "Serge always gets the brides down the aisle. He's so good at keeping them calm."

Hope couldn't imagine the excitable alien ever being calm, but she took Reina by the shoulders. "And you'll be just as good. All you have to do is think of Serge. What would Serge do?"

Reina blinked a few times, then straightened her shoulders. "You're right. I can be Serge if I have to." She put one hand on her hip and snapped her bony fingers. "Cerise, don't just stand there like a bump on a log. You hold the train, and I'll carry the bouquet."

Hope cocked an eyebrow at Cerise, who just shrugged. To be fair, that did sound like something the bossy Gatazoid would say.

Reina plucked the bouquet out of the box, holding it carefully by the ribbon-wrapped handle, and strode toward the door, glancing over her shoulder and beckoning them to follow. "Come on, ladies. You're moving slower than pond water."

"Serge does like his Earth expressions," Cerise muttered, as she took Hope's train. "I hadn't realized how much I *didn't* miss them until now."

"They may be Earth expressions, but they aren't from my part of Earth," Hope told her, keeping her voice low so Reina couldn't hear. "As long as they help Reina, I'm fine with them."

Reina led them out of the suite and down the hall. Xarla stood outside a set of double doors, wearing a mocha-colored dress that played beautifully off her gold skin. She held a clutch of fuchsia flowers in one hand and her tail in the other.

"How's my maid of honor?" Hope asked.

"Confused," Xarla admitted. "My duties are not what I would expect of a maid."

Reina tapped a foot on the floor. "Don't make me explain it again, sweetie. You just walk and smile."

"I'm having serious doubts about this whole 'channeling Serge' thing," Cerise mumbled behind Hope.

Reina peeked inside the double doors and waved at someone before pulling her head back out. "This is it. They're starting your music."

She tugged Xarla forward and pushed her through the door, calling after her, "Walk and smile, hon. That's right. Walk and smile."

Pulling her head back out and closing the door, Reina positioned Hope so she stood in the middle of the closed doors, giving her a quick once-over and handing her the bouquet. She took a deep breath. "Ready?"

Was she? She'd been too distracted by Reina's impersonation of Serge to be nervous herself, but as she felt Cerise unfurl the train behind her and the first muffled notes of wedding music drifted out of the room, her pulse quickened.

This was it. She was actually getting married to an alien warrior she'd only met a little over a week ago, something she'd sworn up and down she'd never do. Then again, she'd done a lot of things she never imagined she'd do, including fly in a spaceship and meet more different types of aliens than she could have ever dreamt existed.

Hope thought about Kos, and her body heated. As strange as it was, she didn't feel any doubt when it came to him. The only thing she felt when she thought about spending the rest of her life with him was excitement.

"I'm ready," she said, smiling at Reina and Cerise, who now stood on either side of the double doors.

Reina nodded at the tiny alien with pink hair, and the two opened the doors at the same time.

Hope stood still for a moment, catching her breath and taking in the scene. The room was long, with a high ceiling and chairs lining both sides, and an aisle down the middle. Reina may not have had holographic technology to work with, but she'd outdone herself with what she'd had.

Tall poles stood at the side of each row of chairs, with a garland of white flowers draping across to the other side, creating a long floral canopy for her to walk under. At the end of the aisle was a large circle of more white flowers suspended from the ceiling. And under that stood her groom.

When she saw him, standing tall in his dark dress uniform, with a decorated sash across one shoulder, she forgot to breathe. Damn, he was gorgeous, and, she thought with some amount of satisfaction, he was all hers.

Kos met her gaze down the aisle, and his face broke into a smile. Even from across the room, Hope could see his eyes glistening.

"You need to start walking, hon," Reina whispered, poking her head out from behind the door.

"Right. Sorry. Thanks for everything." Hope blew a kiss at Reina, who promptly burst into tears.

Hope started walking down the aisle, the music drowning out the sound of Reina's sobbing behind her. Even though the room was filled with guests—lots of Drexian warriors she knew were friends of her fiancé, along with a decent number of human women who were obviously tribute brides, and even Vexlings and Gatazoids she guessed must be other wedding planners and liaisons—she kept her gaze locked on Kos. As long as she focused on him, the crowd of strangers looking at her didn't make her nervous. When he held her gaze with his gray eyes, everything else disappeared.

Hope reached the front of the aisle and took his hand, and heat pulsed through her from his touch.

"You look beautiful, *cinnara*," he whispered.

"You too," she said, with a trembling giggle.

Deep throat clearing made them both look forward. She hadn't realized until that moment that Captain Varden was performing their ceremony, but she smiled when she saw the distinguished Drexian standing in front of them.

"Shall we?" he asked, his smile warm.

Kos and Hope looked at each other, and he squeezed her hand.

"Hell, yeah," she said.

EPILOGUE

Captain Brok stalked along the metal corridor of the Inferno Force ship, his thick-soled boots pounding on the floor as he made his way to the bridge. His ship smelled of stale booze and sweat, even more so since they'd been flying for a while without stopping for his men to disembark and let off steam. There was no time for that now. Not when they were on a mission.

Moisture still beaded on his temple from his workout in the gym, and his muscles twitched from being pushed to their limits. He scraped a hand through his long, dark hair as he reached the bridge, and his officers turned, thumping their fists on their chests in salute.

He returned their salute quickly, catching the eye of his first officer before he turned back to his console. "Report."

"We heard from our sister ship, but the Pregarian outpost was a dead end."

Brok grunted as he began to pace across the back of the bridge. He looked out the wide glass fronting the bridge; nothing but the vast blackness of space as they searched for the missing tribute brides and the Gatazoid wedding planner. It had been weeks since they started the hunt, and so far they'd only found the Vexling and one of the tributes, sending the pretty human back to Drexian space with her mate.

His warriors shifted restlessly at their standing consoles. They were as impatient as he was. Inferno Force was accustomed to battles, not drawn-out searches across a galaxy that seemed endless.

"We will find them," he said, reassuring himself as much as his warriors. "No one evades Inferno Force forever."

Low murmurs of agreement did nothing to make him feel better. He strode to the back of the bridge, touching a hand to the transparent, wall-sized star chart and causing it to illuminate. Crossing his thick arms, the captain studied the path they'd taken.

When they'd located the human female being held by the Ganthar pirates, he'd been able to persuade them—aided by an unexpected uprising and prison break within the ship—to reveal the names of the aliens the other prisoners had been sold to. Unfortunately, he'd only been given names, and tracking down individuals throughout the galaxy was easier said than done. Especially since the type of individuals to buy slaves from Ganthar pirates weren't the type to advertise their whereabouts.

He shook his head as he thought back to the outposts they'd checked and all the seedy criminals they'd interrogated. By now, the sector must be buzzing with word that Inferno Force was looking for slaves sold by Ganthar pirates. That would either help flush out the culprits or drive them further underground.

"Doesn't matter," Brok muttered to himself. "I'll find them eventually."

He never gave up, especially when it came to helping others. It was why he made such a good captain. He had no problem sacrificing himself for the greater good of Inferno Force, and he'd done just that many times in battle. He subconsciously touched the scar that scored one side of his face—a souvenir from a battle against the Kronock in which he'd fought off the enemy to let the other ships escape and barely escaped with his own life.

He had no regrets. It was what Inferno Force did. It was why they were known as the toughest and roughest warriors anywhere in the galaxy. If his scars made him appear frightening, so much the better. The only reason he'd need to be handsome would be if he wanted to take a tribute bride, but he'd never put himself on the list. Inferno Force was his family.

No, it was better for him out on the outskirts of space with his Inferno Force crew. He dropped his hand from the thin scar. He would not subject a pretty, fragile human female to a battle-scarred warrior like him, even if there was one who could look at him without flinching.

"Captain." Kalex joined him at the star chart, inclining his head briefly before tapping a point on the clear map. "What about the lead we got on Doxvane?"

"From that drunk?" Brok shook his head. "We don't have any indication that his information wasn't a whiskey-fueled hallucination."

"True." Kalex rocked back on his heels. "But his story never changed. Even when he dried out. A human female and a Gatazoid en route to the planet Spartos."

The captain squinted at a blue dot on the map. "Spartos hasn't had contact with other species in generations. They're famously xenophobic. Why would they suddenly be buying slaves from pirates?"

"I agree it doesn't make sense, but remember that our source said the Spartosians didn't make the purchase themselves. They bought the human and Gatazoid through an emissary."

Brok let out a breath. He'd been thinking about the bit of intel since they'd interrogated the washed-up drunk. His tip was the only one they'd gotten in a while, but it also seemed the most far-fetched.

"It still doesn't explain why a planet that makes a point of never interacting with the outside universe would suddenly be buying aliens," Brok said. "They believe all other species to be inferior. The thought of a human and a Gatazoid even being allowed to set foot on their planet is crazy."

"Agreed." Kalex folded his arms over his chest, the thick bands of tattoos flashing from under the sleeve of his black T-shirt. "But what if Spartos has changed? It's been a millennium since anyone has interacted with them."

"And you think that change is to suddenly buy alien slaves?"

Kalex shrugged. "It's the only lead we have. Our other ships are coming up empty, too. It's like these females have vanished into thin air."

Brok scowled as he stared at the star chart. The warrior was right. That was exactly how it felt, and Brok's frustration was growing to the point where he felt he wanted to break something. He glanced down at his raw knuckles. Hence the intense sessions with the punching bag.

The Drexians were responsible for the humans they took from Earth. They'd vowed to protect them, not let them be kidnapped by pirates and then sold into who knew what kind of situation. His stomach clenched as he thought of how long the females had been missing.

"You are right," he said. "We have to pursue it, even if it's another dead end."

"Shall I set a course for Spartos?" Kalex asked, his eyes sparking with anticipation.

Captain Brok gave him a curt nod, and the warrior spun on his heel and returned to his post.

"Setting a course for Spartos," Kalex bellowed behind him.

The other warriors shouted their agreement, pounding their feet on the floor and making the bridge shake. Brok tried to share in their excitement, but a hard knot had settled in his gut.

Even if Spartos did have the prisoners, how would they get

them back? The planet did not allow aliens to enter their atmosphere, and there was no diplomat to send their request to. If they found the human and Gatazoid, they would have to track them down using stealth and sneak them out without being seen. He knew from experience this was easier said than done.

It didn't matter, he reminded himself. The human female and Gatazoid were under Drexian protection, and it was his sworn duty to find them. He would not fail. He never failed.

Clenching his fists, he pivoted to face the front of the bridge. His chest swelled with pride as he looked across at the Inferno Force warriors faithfully manning their posts—his family. Their hair was longer than most Drexians wore it, they had considerably more ink than other Drexians, and most boasted considerably more scars. He had served with some of these warriors since he'd assumed command and he thought of them as brothers. The brothers he'd never had in his own family.

There had been much he had not had in his family growing up. Not after his father had been injured in battle. Instead of dying a warrior's death, he had not succumbed to his injures. He had lingered, wasting away slowly. Brok had become the leader of the family when he was only ten solar rotations, and he had been taking care of family ever since.

He swallowed the bitter taste of bile that always rose in his throat when he thought of his family. They were all gone now, but the pain lingered. The pain that he had not been able to save them no matter how hard he'd tried.

His fingers bit into his palms. He had not failed since. Not after joining Inferno Force. And he would not fail now.

"I will find you," he whispered, envisioning the image of the human they were tracking.

His crew had been shown the images of all the missing tribute brides, and he knew the pictures of the pretty females had served to motivate his warriors. He suspected some imagined taking one of

179

them for themselves, although no one knew if the remaining females were already matched or not. That knowledge wouldn't stop his warriors from envisioning themselves with the humans. He suspected the mental images had kept many of the Drexians company in their racks at night, and he could not fault them for it, even though jealousy coursed through him if he thought about any other Drexian thinking about *her*.

He knew she wasn't his, but he needed to keep the female they were searching for in his mind, so he knew who he was fighting for. That wasn't hard, since the female's dark eyes had seemed to burn into his soul the moment he'd seen them.

The female that the pirates claimed they'd sold along with the Gatazoid was the smallest of the females—the runt, they called her. But Brok couldn't stop thinking about her dark hair, golden skin, and slightly upturned eyes—the combination something he'd never seen before. Although, as the captain of an Inferno Force ship who'd never been to the Boat, he hadn't seen many humans and didn't have much to compare her to. Still, he'd found her picture mesmerizing.

Brok repeated her name in his mind, finally saying it under his breath, almost as if it were a prayer. "Madeleine."

None of his warriors heard him. They were too focused on setting their new course, the computers beeping as they tapped fingers across their consoles. The captain steadied his breathing as he thought about her, his pulse quickening and his cock swelling, despite his best efforts.

He knew his desire was a distraction he couldn't afford, but he had been unable to rid himself of it no matter how much time he spent with the punching bag. It was not as if the human would ever want a scarred creature like him. He would never expect her to. Not when there were hundreds of perfect, handsome Drexians waiting for a bride. It didn't matter, he told himself, pushing aside his arousal.

He would find Madeleine, and he would take her back to the Boat. That was his job, and he would do it.

A muscle ticked on the side of his jaw as he tried not to think about what would happen next. That wasn't his concern. She wasn't his tribute bride. She was only his to save.

And he would save her. No matter the cost.

THANK you for reading Hope and Kos's story! Up next for the Drexian Warriors? Captain Brok's story in SCARRED, book 10 of the Tribute Brides of the Drexian Warriors series.

One Click SCARRED Now>>

"Brok is the dream alien I've always wanted...and for most of the book he's running around in his boxers briefs. Yes, ladies, the book gods have gifted us with delicious male warrior mostly naked while carrying out a rescue mission!"-Amazon Reviewer

WANT to read about some sexy alien barbarians? You'll love BOUNTY, the first book in Tana Stone's Barbarians of the Sand Planet series.

After crash-landing in an unfamiliar desert, human Danica is rescued by gorgeous, telepathic alien K'alvek. And while he vows to help her bounty hunter crew escape the hostile planet, he can't subdue his burning desire to claim his new charge.

One-click BOUNTY Now>

"This was excellent! I could not put it down. The world building is amazing and the characters are likable and as always Tana knows how to make it super steamy."-Amazon Reviewer

This book has been edited and proofed, but typos are like little gremlins that like to sneak in when we're not looking. If you spot a typo, please report it to: tana@tanastone.com
Thank you!!

PREVIEW OF BOUNTY— BARBARIANS OF THE SAND PLANET #1

Below is a sample of another Tana Stone sci-fi-romance series—this one with alien barbarians and female bounty hunters!

Chapter One

"Are they shooting at us?" Danica asked, grabbing the edge of a smooth, metal console as she stepped onto the bridge and the ship heaved to one side. She tasted blood as she bit the inside of her mouth, and flinched from the pain. *Son of a bitch.*

She and Bexli had just brought their latest captive onboard, and she'd given the order to take off, hoping the rival bounty hunters who'd also been in pursuit hadn't seen them. From the staccato sounds of gunfire, she guessed that her plan of slipping out unnoticed was shot to hell.

She took in the familiar sight of the compact bridge—a round, flat panel console in the center of the room with view screens suspended above it, smaller individual consoles forming a half moon around the main one, and a final ring of screened consoles against the circular walls. A long, narrow slit of a window gave them a view out the front of the ship, but had a steel shade they could lower for security. Nearly every part of the room was composed of metal that was long past gleaming, and looked nearly black with age and grime. Wires spilled from underneath most of the consoles, a result of various hacks and patches to keep the aging space ship running. Danica inhaled the scent of burning fuel that seemed to permeate the ship, and felt a rush of affection for the bucket of bolts she'd practically grown up on.

"Looks like it," her pilot, Caro, said turning from one of the smaller consoles where she navigated the ship, her straight, nearly black hair flying behind her as she spun back around. "And we're definitely outgunned."

"Can we outrun them?" Danica asked, as she made her way down to the center console and looked out at the massive ship blocking their escape.

"What we don't have in size or gun power, we make up for in maneuverability," Caro said. "I should be able to get a little extra acceleration from our impulse drives if I boost the—"

"Caro," Danica said, cutting off the woman before she launched into an overly detailed explanation of their engine.

"Sorry, Captain," Caro said spinning back around to her console. "On it."

"I hope you're right," Tori said from where she stood at the weapons console along the wall, her curly, dark hair pulled up in a topknot and held in place with what looked like metal chopsticks with dangerously sharp ends—almost as sharp as her pointy teeth. A row of hard, raised bumps ran above her eyebrows, down along the sides of her face and disappeared into her hairline—a hallmark of the Zevrians—making her look even fiercer than she was. "Because we're running low on weapons."

"How low?" Danica gripped the console with both hands as the ship jerked to the right and skirted underneath the larger ship.

"How good are you at hand-to-hand combat?" Tori asked, her brown, muscled arms braced against the wall.

Danica had gotten a lot of flak—mostly from her father's old bounty-hunter friends—when she'd brought on the Zevrian as her security chief, but she'd never had a moment's regret for making Tori a part of her team. Especially in situations like these.

"I thought we were supposed to stock up when we were docked at Centuri Twelve," Danica shouted over the roar of the engines firing.

"I would have, if we had anything to buy them with," Tori said as the ship accelerated.

Danica sighed. Her crew had been running on fumes—sometimes literally—for weeks. "I know it's been tight, but once we turn over this bounty, we'll flush for a while."

"I'm just glad Mourad won't have the satisfaction of beating us." Caro turned to face forward as the force of acceleration pressed her back into her chair. "I hate that guy."

Danica couldn't agree more. The ship shooting at them belonged to a bounty hunter and mercenary named Mourad, who didn't believe in female bounty hunters and didn't believe in playing fair. Not that Danica was against stretching the rules or pushing her luck, but Mourad had no limits on what he and his crew would do to capture a bounty.

He was the one bounty hunter her father had gone out of his way to avoid, because Mourad ignored all the usual professional courtesies and accepted practices. He would double-cross anyone. Instead of tracking down bounties himself, he was known for waiting until another bounty hunter did all the legwork, then he and his band of mercenaries would swoop in and snake the bounty. Just like he was trying to do now.

Over my dead body, Danica thought, as their ship broke through the atmosphere and shot into space, the sky going from hazy yellow to inky blue to black. She thumped the side of the console, mentally thanking the ship for getting her out of yet another scrape.

When her father died, he'd left everything to her, which meant basically his ship. It had just been the three of them for as long as Danica could remember—her and her father and the ship. Different crews had come and gone, but the ship had been the only constant in their lives, aside from each other. She'd thought about selling it, but only for a moment. The old ship was as much a part of her as her father had been, and she couldn't stand the thought of losing both of them.

She knew her father had never wanted her to take over his bounty-hunting business. Truth be told, he never thought it was possible, but after spending a childhood chasing after crooks all over the galaxy, she didn't really know any other life. She was good at tracking people and getting out of scrapes and skirting the law. Her father had taught her well.

Danica shook thoughts of her father out of her head as she glanced at the fuel gauge. "Good work. We should have enough steam to reach the Gendarvian outpost, where we can unload our bounty and get our reward."

Tori crossed the bridge to stand next to her, the chain belt wrapped several times around her waist jingling as she walked. "I wonder what this one did to command such a high price."

Danica shrugged, tucking a loose strand of wavy, blonde hair behind her ear. "It's not our business to wonder why. I can tell you it wasn't for a violent offense. I've never had a bounty put up less of a fight."

"The tracking was the hard part. Dr. Max Dryden did a fucking brilliant job of hiding."

The women turned to see their engineer, Holly, step onto the bridge. While the rest of Danica's crew favored utilitarian clothes that made them look more like their male counterparts—military issue pants, T-shirts, multi-pocketed vests and jackets—the ship's engineer and resident computer whiz wore color and patterns and combined them fearlessly. Red hair spilled over her shoulders and down the skintight, pink-paisley top she'd paired over an equally snug pair of turquoise pants. Her decidedly feminine appearance didn't do a thing to stop her from cursing like a space pirate, which usually startled people who thought her girly looks meant she was all sugar and spice.

"Not good enough to outfox us," Tori said, hand on her hip.

"Luckily for you, I understand the doctor's research and narrowed it down to the few planets that are ideal for that type of scientific study," Holly said. "And then Bexli did her thing."

Bexli was the other non-human in the crew. A Lycithian shape-shifter who excelled at sneaking in and out of otherwise impenetrable places, she was their ace in the hole. Officially, she was their acquisitions officer, but only in the sense that she could acquire any bounty by way of her shape-shifting skills. She was so indispensable, Danica even put up with the pet glurkin that Bexli had insisted on bringing on board.

"Remind me again what type of research," Tori said, then shook her head. "Never mind, I actually don't care."

Holly rolled her eyes at Tori. "The study of a rare mineral only found in a few systems. Word on the astronet is that the doctor has figured out a way to harness its power, which would be fucking amazing."

Caro twisted in her chair to face them. "I'm still not thrilled we're turning over a scientist. Are we sure this is a legit bounty? How many doctors do you know who commit crimes severe enough to command this amount? Should we really be turning in other women? I mean, we're an all female bounty-hunting crew."

Danica frowned, partly at Caro's barrage of questions and partly because she'd had the same thoughts, and had been trying to ignore her inner voice during the entire search. "We don't have the luxury of picking and choosing our bounties. Anyway, if we don't turn the doctor in, someone else will. At least we treat our prisoners well."

"Not that all of them deserve it." Tori pulled up the hem of her black cargo pants to reveal a thin, red scar running up her calf. "We should have put that Daxian smuggler out the airlock."

"Agreed," Bexli said, as she joined the other women on the

bridge, a tiny puff of green fur running along beside her. "He was particularly repulsive."

"Is the bounty all settled?" Danica asked.

Bexli nodded, and her iridescent-lavender bob swung at her jawbone. "This one was a breeze. I didn't even have to transform into something terrifying to keep her in line."

She leaned against a console and scooped Pog up in one arm, ruffling its fur and making it emit a low purr. "The Daxian from our last mission only stopped struggling when I morphed into a gorvon."

"Remind me again, what's a gorvon?" Holly asked.

"A particularly gruesome creature from the Daxian's home world." Bexli grinned. "Lots of claws and fangs."

Caro laughed, tightening her high ponytail. "That explains why he soiled his cell."

"At least he kept us in fuel and rations for a month," Danica said, glancing at Tori. "And you gave him a few scars, if I remember correctly."

Tori grinned. "A souvenir from the bounty hunter babes."

"You know I hate that nickname." Danica folded her arms across her chest.

"Babes is better than the other name they call us that also starts with a *b*." Holly leaned against one of the consoles, crossing her long legs at the ankles.

"I don't mind the name so much," Caro said. "At least they're talking about us."

Danica let out a long breath. "They should be talking about us because we've brought in the two highest bounties in the past astro-year, not because we're all women."

Holly patted her on the shoulder. "It's just because we're the first—and so far only—all-female bounty-hunter crew. Once the novelty wears off, or another crew comes along, people will talk about something else."

Danica knew there was truth in Holly's words, but she hated the

fact that even though they'd brought in two of the toughest bounties around, the other hunters still didn't respect them. She'd
known working in a field known for tough guys wouldn't be easy,
but she'd hoped her unorthodox methods and maverick crew would
win her respect. So far, they'd only managed to acquire nicknames.

"I say we own it," Tori said, taking one of the pointy chopsticks
from her hair and pressing the needle-like point into the pad of her
finger. "We know we can do any job the boys can do and, once we
bring in this hot-shot doctor, we'll be rolling in enough dough to
outfit this ship so we can blast anyone out of the sky. Let them call
us babes then."

"Um, guys." Caro's fingers flew across the screen in front of her.
"We probably shouldn't count our money quite yet."

Danica jerked her head to the screens above her, slamming her
palm against the console when she saw the rival ship closing in on
them. "I thought we had enough of a head start to lose them."

"They're faster than I expected for a ship that large," Caro said,
maneuvering their ship so that it dipped to the left.

Holly slid onto the floor, landing with a thud. "A little warning
next time."

"Sorry," Caro shouted over the sound of weapons fire hitting
their hull. "You should probably brace for impact."

A blast shook the ship and alarms began screaming, red lights
flashing overhead.

"Was that a torpedo?" Danica asked, shaking her head in disbelief. Was a rival bounty hunter really trying to blow up her ship?

"Shit." Holly scrambled to her feet, using the nearest console to
pull herself toward the door. "I'd better get back to the engine room.
If we lose that, we're dead in the water."

"I'll go make sure the prisoner is okay," Bexli said, following
Holly with Pog tucked under one arm.

The entire ship jolted, and Danica heard the sound of metal
scraping against metal. Her skin went cold. "They've clamped on."

Tori's face was grim. "They're boarding us."

"Maybe they'll take the doctor and go," Caro said, although her voice quivered. Danica knew her pilot had been captured more than once when she was a pilot for a resistance movement, and she suspected it hadn't always been pleasant.

Danica squeezed her hands into fists. "They're not taking our bounty or us." She turned to Tori. "Hold them off as long as you can, but don't get yourself killed. I have a plan."

Tori pulled the other chopstick from her hair and slipped both sharp metal sticks into her chain belt. "You got it, Captain."

Danica ran off the bridge and down the dimly lit corridor until she reached a steel door where Bexli stood guard. "I've got the doctor. Why don't you and Pog try to hold off Mourad's soldiers?"

Bexli nodded, her lithe frame and lavender hair transforming into a hulking beast covered in matted fur, with only the slightest hint of purple at the tips. Pog gave a gruff bark and became a green lizard the size of a human, with short legs that scampered across the floor. Both creatures hurried off toward the noise of the enemy bounty hunters boarding their ship.

Danica turned back to the steel door and punched in a code. The door slid open with a groan, revealing a petite figure with short, chocolate-brown hair sitting on the edge of a cot in the sparse room.

"Doctor Dryden," Danica said, her breath ragged. "Some pretty nasty bounty hunters are coming on board to take you. I can promise you they won't be as humane as we've been, but I have a plan that could save us both."

The woman on the cot blinked her wide, blue eyes a few times before answering. "Call me Max."

To be continued . . .

Want to read BOUNTY, book 1 in the Barbarians of the Sand Planet series? Click HERE to keep reading!

ALSO BY TANA STONE

The Tribute Brides of the Drexian Warriors Series:

TAMED (also available in AUDIO)

SEIZED (also available in AUDIO)

EXPOSED (also available in AUDIO)

RANSOMED (also available in AUDIO)

FORBIDDEN (also available in AUDIO)

BOUND (also available in AUDIO)

JINGLED (A Holiday Novella) (also in AUDIO)

CRAVED (also available in AUDIO)

STOLEN (also available in AUDIO)

SCARRED (also available in AUDIO)

ALIEN & MONSTER ONE-SHOTS:

ROGUE (also available in AUDIO)

VIXIN: STRANDED WITH AN ALIEN

SLIPPERY WHEN YETI

CHRISTMAS WITH AN ALIEN

YOOL

Raider Warlords of the Vandar Series:

POSSESSED (also available in AUDIO)

PLUNDERED (also available in AUDIO)

PILLAGED (also available in AUDIO)

PURSUED (also available in AUDIO)

PUNISHED (also available on AUDIO)

PROVOKED (also available in AUDIO)

PRODIGAL (also available in AUDIO)

PRISONER

PROTECTOR

PRINCE

The Barbarians of the Sand Planet Series:

BOUNTY (also available in AUDIO)

CAPTIVE (also available in AUDIO)

TORMENT (also available on AUDIO)

TRIBUTE (also available as AUDIO)

SAVAGE (also available in AUDIO)

CLAIM (also available on AUDIO)

CHERISH: A Holiday Baby Short (also available on AUDIO)

PRIZE (also available on AUDIO)

SECRET

RESCUE (appearing first in PETS IN SPACE #8)

Inferno Force of the Drexian Warriors:

IGNITE (also available on AUDIO)

SCORCH (also available on AUDIO)

BURN (also available on AUDIO)

BLAZE (also available on AUDIO)

FLAME (also available on AUDIO)

COMBUST

THE SKY CLAN OF THE TAORI:

SUBMIT (also available in AUDIO)

STALK (also available on AUDIO)

SEDUCE (also available on AUDIO)

SUBDUE

STORM

All the TANA STONE books available as audiobooks!

INFERNO FORCE OF THE DREXIAN WARRIORS:

IGNITE on AUDIBLE

SCORCH on AUDIBLE

BURN on AUDIBLE

BLAZE on AUDIBLE

FLAME on AUDIBLE

RAIDER WARLORDS OF THE VANDAR:

POSSESSED on AUDIBLE

PLUNDERED on AUDIBLE

PILLAGED on AUDIBLE

PURSUED on AUDIBLE

PUNISHED on AUDIBLE

PROVOKED on AUDIBLE

BARBARIANS OF THE SAND PLANET

BOUNTY on AUDIBLE

CAPTIVE on AUDIBLE

TORMENT on AUDIBLE

TRIBUTE on AUDIBLE

SAVAGE on AUDIBLE

CLAIM on AUDIBLE

CHERISH on AUDIBLE

TRIBUTE BRIDES OF THE DREXIAN WARRIORS

TAMED on AUDIBLE

SEIZED on AUDIBLE

EXPOSED on AUDIBLE

RANSOMED on AUDIBLE

FORBIDDEN on AUDIBLE

BOUND on AUDIBLE

JINGLED on AUDIBLE

CRAVED on AUDIBLE

STOLEN on AUDIBLE

SCARRED on AUDIBLE

SKY CLAN OF THE TAORI

SUBMIT on AUDIBLE

STALK on AUDIBLE

SEDUCE on AUDIBLE

About the Author

Tana Stone is a USA Today bestselling sci-fi romance author who loves sexy aliens and independent heroines. Her favorite superhero is Thor (with Aquaman a close second because, well, Jason Momoa), her favorite dessert is key lime pie (okay, fine, *all* pie), and she loves Star Wars and Star Trek equally. She still laments the loss of *Firefly*.

She has one husband, two teenagers, and two neurotic cats. She sometimes wishes she could teleport to a holographic space station like the one in her tribute brides series (or maybe vacation at the oasis with the sand planet barbarians). :-)

She loves hearing from readers! Email her any questions or comments at tana@tanastone.com.

Want to join her VIP Readers list and be the first to know about contests and giveaways? Click here: BookHip.com/CRJHNH

Want to hang out with Tana in her private Facebook group? Join on all the fun at: https://www.facebook.com/groups/tanastonestributes/

Printed in Dunstable, United Kingdom